BROOKLYNN HEAT
IN MIAMI

BY LUCY CULT

This book is dedicated to my readers, because of your kind words, and support I was able to finish this book. All of you are what keeps me writing, so Thank You.

Lucy Cult

Brooklynn Heat In Miami

Cover design Robert L. Cantrell III

For further information log onto LiberatedBohemian@wix.com

ATT: Liberated Bohemian c/o Lucy Cult

2451 NW 63rd ave Sunrise, Fl. 33313

ISBN 13: 9780615814384

ISBN 10: 0615814387

Library of Congress has been applied for

Acknowledgements

First of all I would like to thank my Heavenly Father up above for his guidance and healing halo over me that allow me to continue to get my stories out.

To my lovely kids, I love y'all so much, there are not enough words to express the happiness and love you all have filled in my life, I will continue to build this foundation for all of you.

To my supporters, readers, especially Ashley Joyce and Jada Marie, your support has been much appreciated. With people like you in my life makes my job easier. Thank you for everything.

Again I would like to thank my family and friends from Bloomfield Ct. to Ft. Lauderdale Fl. For all the love and support that you have brought into my life Thank You.

Contents:

The first time I saw him was at the gas station, I just drove up to put gas in the tank of my car, and saw him standing there on the side of his car, sizing me up and down. I didn't look away, couldn't look away, and something about him was intriguing to me. Was it his stance or his lips that drew me near to him? No, it was his eyes, umm those dreamy sleepy looking eyes, nothing else, I was in a trance, our eyes met and he had me. Not to let him know that I was about to say yes to anything that came out of his mouth, I quickly try to focus on something else. I started to look for a way out of my hypnosis and saw a Black n Mild cigar resting on top of his ear making him more suave to me. "You have another one of those I can have?" I opened my mouth and the words came out just like I wanted it to, sexy, flirtatious, and enticing. "No, this is my last one, but you can definitely have this one." He answered back with a smile that set a chill up and down my spine making my body feel warm and tingly as if I just drank a glass of dry wine, taking the cigar off of his ear and gracefully handing it to me, letting me know that he was willing to give me whatever I wanted at that moment, and in my case what I needed. I took it from him and smiled back starting to head to the inside of the gas station store and I can almost feel his eyes watching me as I walked away, but I refuse to turn back in fear of stumbling in front of me to reveal my vulnerability towards him. Returning to my car, I noticed he had not left even though he was done pumping gas. "I couldn't leave without asking you if your busy tomorrow night?" He was so smooth talking about approaching me with a line that I couldn't just brush him off as I have done in the past to other strange men, but his eyes once again lured me in hook, line, and sinker. "I have no plans, as *YET*." I emphasized on the YET, giving him all the ammunition he needed to proceed to reel me in. "If I give you my number can you, no, will you make sure to use it? I'm Chrome by the way." Handing me a slip of paper he already had filled out while I was in the store so sure of himself. I didn't hesitate to take it. "Chrome huh? And is that your real name or just what your friends call you?" Not promising to use his number but instead to have him anticipating by his phone for my call, was just my way of taking back control of this hold he seem to have over me. "No, Chrome is just for you." Damn, I thought, he got me, I'm done, I had to laugh at my own self for getting caught up now, when I look back at what I could have walked away from, I might not be in all this <u>Heat.</u>

CHAPTER 1 DISENGAGEMENT

Slamming my jeep door, stepping away from him was all I could do to stop me from slapping the shit out of my x. We have been together since our high school days, inseparable, and yet never went outside of our relationship. Always stayed true to each other, and even though we had no kids, and we weren't married, everybody knew we were together. So why is it now that we are having issues, arguing all the time, about infidelity.

"Damn, I knew this would happen, the day I sat and waited on you to come get me from work, and you talking bout you fell asleep at your boys house, hell naw, you was with that Bitch weren't you?"

I cursed him out waiting for an answer, even though I knew the answer already. You see Tony had been acting different ever since we left a party that he DJ for. It was a regular Miami pool party hosted by some dude they call Heat, for his wifey's birthday,

Tony Vice, one of Miami's best D.J.'s which was a plus for me, since I could get into any club for free, but at this party the hoochie mama's were all out, and the dawgs were ready to play. Tony never cheated on me before and I never on him, so I thought I had nothing to worry about when my girl Kat was ready to leave before the party was over, I was her ride, and Tony had his truck so he was ok to get home, but this one hoe stepped out of the house with nothing but a G-string all in one bathing suit on and a slit all the way down in the front, blond weave all down her back, and long ass nails, you have to wonder how she wash her coochie with them nails. Ladies all know her from the club as a gold digging whore, whoever pockets were fatter in the club she was going home with him that night. Well that day she was scoping out Tony, he was getting paid twenty five thousand dollars for the party, and I'm pretty sure, now that I look back she knew exactly how much he was getting paid.

"I don't know what you are talking about, this was a one niter mistake, it was not my intention, there had to be something in my drink. Baby you know I don't get down like that. It was a moment of weakness, drinking, and smoking, she had to have slipped me something."

Tony pleaded, trying to take the denial road, but I wasn't falling for it, had the tables been turned I would've never heard the end of it. My Dad always told me, if a man cheats on you once he will do it again, and if he puts his hands you once it will never be that one time, and just in case he had a twelve gage shotgun waiting for him in the hallway closet. Dad didn't raise no fool, even though my Mom was always there for me with girl talk, Dad is the one who taught me how to fin for myself and take no shit from anyone.

"Look, all I know is the last thing I ever thought would happen, is for me to walk in and see you all laid up with that Bitch, and what kind of name is Sugar Cane anyway? She doesn't look all that sweet to me. Whatever, it's over, and I'm done, you've hurt me and I can't look at you right now, so this is good bye Tony, hope she was worth losing me."

Trying to hold back the tears from falling in front of him, I pulled him out of my two thousand ten candy apple green, twenty six inch Chrome rims, Wrangler, my birthday present from Tony one year, and he wasn't getting it back.

"Wait up Brooklynn Baby, you can't leave like this, and you can't leave me here without a ride back home either, just calm down and let's work this shit out."

He said as I got in my ride, locking the doors and pulling away, hell who cares if we were twenty seven miles out on the highway away from home, he didn't need my help cheating on me he don't need my help finding a way home, besides I left him with his legs still attached he can WALK home for all I care. No second chances, no more waiting home all hours of the night till he thought I was sleeping to sneak in, no more unknown calls on his locked cell phone that never use to be lock before, there was NO MORE US!

As I pulled up into our driveway of our five bedroom two story brownstone on Coconut Grove that he had built for us, just because I always love the brownstones in New York, I started to wonder, was I doing the right thing, and was there really no getting past this? I already knew the answer in my heart that was shattered and broken, I had sisters that was going through this same shit and friends that could tolerate the bullshit, but I couldn't, and I wasn't going to let him get one over on me. It's his house now, he can keep it as a reminder of what he threw away when he dropped his pants and let another Bitch taste him. Pulling out my Burberry designer suitcases was hard for me, the only time I would pull these out was when Tony had a big DJ Clash to go to out of town or state, now I'm pulling them out to pack all my stuff, and go, but not before I went to Tony's safe he built behind his nine thousand gallon cylinder filled with exotic fishes and coral reef, it stood from downstairs all the way to the top of our house imaging a stripper pole but it was breath taking, I will definitely miss it. I opened up the safe that had to have about six hundred g's in it maybe even more, Tony had several safes with money it, one at his Moms, one here where we lived, one at his Sisters house in Coral Gables, and about two more in the Islands somewhere, he didn't trust banks, and he never kept all in one place in fear of being robbed. I wasn't going to be greedy or hurt him that bad, besides I was keeping the Jeep he paid off on, and the clothes, and the jewelry he gave me over the years, hell he wasn't getting back the fourteen karat Canary Diamond necklace he just got me for Valentine's day I chuckled to myself as I took it out of the safe, and of course I knew the combination to his safe, he would've told me anyway, but I let him think he had that secrete to himself. Taking only about two hundred and fifty grand was enough for me to get my own place and chill till I can figure out what my next step was.

For the first couple of nights I stayed at The Executive Hotel near the Airport. I wasn't ready just yet to start looking for a new home because I still was hurt by Tony and his infidelity, that a hotel room with closed shades, and a bottle of Hennessey VSOP was my only comfort. Lying down on the bed was nothing like our king size pillow top bed, my head was spinning from the liquor and from the situation I now found myself in when I started to feel a soothing vibration. It was my cell phone, and Kat's name was lighting up.

"Yeah?"

I answered not really in the mood to talk to anyone or handle Kat's call. Katrina Neive, Brazilian nut complexion and a curvaceous slim body, who goes by the name Kat, has been my friend since we were lil jits growing up in Miami. From the sandbox to the table dancing, she was a wild one, and full of life, we always kept it real with each other and I never had anything to worry about when it came to Tony. You see Kat loves kitty kat, she plays for the other team, and she likes other girls, fems and the butches. She likes living in the moment, never thinking about tomorrow, and never settling down with one person always on the move, loving the night life, I just hope she wasn't calling to go out tonight.

"Brooklynn, now I know you not sitting in no dark room drinking down your miseries? You need to get up and get your game back on."

How did she know I was in a dark room or even drinking? What did she follow me or something?

"How the hell do you know what I'm doing Kat?"

I asked her sitting up in the bed now that she had my full attention.

"Oh Girl, please every time you and Tony would get into an argument back in the days and over lil shit, you would grab a bottle and head for this hotel until things get cool down between y'all." She knew me all so well I thought to myself and had the first smile on my face in days.

"Ohh Kat, I wish this was just one of those times when it was over lil shit, and not over some damn skank ho, but I'm not leaving this room, not yet, he broke my heart real bad."

The tears started to roll down my face once again as I relived this whole nightmare of Tony's betrayal.

"Ok, fine, then we will sit together in your dark room and drink on two bottles of Henn Dawg, open the door because I'm coming up to your room right now." Before I could tell her no, and I will be fine she hung up the phone. I love Kat like she was one of my sisters, and we came from different back ground but we were one in the same. Trying to wash my face and all the evidence off, I hurried and started to straighten up the room, there was tissue paper all over, soaked with salty tears, and just like she said, she was at my door, banging on it and carrying on in the hallway.

"Open this door Brook, you don't want me to cause a scene now do you?" She continued to taunt and play with me, I know she meant well, she always try to keep me smiling.

"Alright, alright, alright, I'm opening the door, don't cause a scene, I have nowhere else to go if they kick me out." I said playfully back to her as I let her in my dungeon of self-pity.

Two days later, I still was sitting on the bed now accompanied by my girl Kat who sat by my side and consoled me, and kept me hydrated between the glasses of cognac with bottles of water and fruit bowls.

"C'mon Brook baby, you can't let this shit get to you, I mean people break up all the time, niggas cheat, that's what they do, hell even I caught a couple of my bitches eating out on the next bitch, and you cry, or fight and get over it. This is not healthy what you doing. Tony hasn't even called you once since you left, he probably fucking that wretched bitch now."
Kat had a point, here I was in my room all day, while his life goes on without me, it was time for me to snap out of it, and if Tony was out getting his it's time for me to get mine. We live in one of the liveliest cities in the country, Miami, full of clubs, and beaches, and it's now or never. I snapped out of my slum, and Kat jumped on the bed like a cheerleader doing her cheer jumps in the air, I shook my head and laughed.

"So glad to see you laughing again Sis, now go on take this and get in that bathroom, go soak your ass in the tub, cuz you have been chilling a lil too long in them jogging pants, and let's get ready to light up the night." Kat handed me a rolled up blunt and pushed me towards the bathroom as she went to sit down at the little table on the balcony to roll another blunt just for her. She always came prepared with joints, never left home without it. The bathroom was soon fogged up with steam from the tub, and my blunt. Sitting down in the hot tub, and inhaling the essence of Kat's purple haze was taking my mind off of everything and soon my head was dancing along with the smoke.

"Don't take all day now Brooklynn, do you need help?" Startling me out of my trance Kat was being inpatient with me.
"Yeah, yeah, ok I'm getting out now." I answered her back, letting the water drain out of the tub. I stepped out of the tub with bubbles falling down my legs, and putting my lil roach out in the ashtray that was on the counter. When I opened the bathroom door, Kat was standing right there holding up a sexy champagne color sleeveless cocktail dress with gold chain straps in the back and a pair of six inch Stiletto heel with gold chain straps to match for me to wear.

"Yeah, that's right I got this in the shop down-stairs in the lobby, and it will look fierce on you. Oh and I got me an outfit too for tonight." She said laying the dress on the bed for me. I couldn't argue it was breathtaking, and her outfit let's just say it was an outlaw red leather tight dress to fit her curvaceous slim body and white platform six inch heel boots.

"You ready girl?" Kat said ready to go.
"Where are we going anyway?"

"Out to South Beach, we can stop at All Stars and have a few drinks and then head over to Casanova's, I have two VIP passes a customer gave me at work." Kat was always receiving free passes and getting invited to all the best parties in the M I A from her job.

"Ok let's go but I have to stop at the gas station first, unless you want to help push in those shoes?" I clowned her walking to my Jeep in the garage of the hotel. We pulled into a gas station right around the corner from the hotel and I got out my jeep to pay for the gas, that's when I saw *HIM*. Standing by his car looking so debonair in his own sinful dark chocolate skin a fresh low cut hair style, wearing a lime green and white strip shirt with a collar and a pair of Coogi jean long shorts, and Birdman Miami Lugs sneakers to finish it off, he had a cool swagga to match those sexy luring eyes of his that took my breath away. He was sizing me up and down, I didn't look away, I couldn't look away, and something about him was intriguing to me, was it his stance or his lips that drew me near to him? No, it was his eyes, umm those dreamy sleepy looking eyes, I saw nothing else, I was in a trance, our eyes met and he had me. Not to let him know that I was about to say yes to anything that came out of his mouth, I quickly try to focus on something else. I started to look for a way out of my hypnosis and saw a Black n Mild cigar resting on top of his ear making him more suave to me.

"You have another one of those I can have?" I opened my mouth and my words came out just like I wanted it to, sexy, flirtatious, and enticing.

"No, this is my last one, but you can definitely have this one." He answered back with a smile that set a chill up and down my spine making my body feel warm and tingly as if I just drank a glass of dry wine, taking the cigar off of his ear and gracefully handing it to me, letting me know that he was willing to give me whatever I wanted at that moment, and in my case what I needed. I took it from him and smiled back starting to head to the inside of the gas station store and I can almost feel his eyes watching me as I walked away, but refusing to turn back in fear of stumbling in front of me to reveal my vulnerability towards him. Returning to my car, I noticed he had not left even though he was done pumping gas.

"I couldn't leave without asking you if your busy tomorrow night?" He was so smooth talking about approaching me with a line that I couldn't just brush him off as I have done in the past to other strange men, but his eyes once again lured me in hook, line, and sinker.

"I have no plans, as YET."

I emphasized on the YET, giving him all the ammunition he needed to proceed to reel me in.

"If I give you my number can you, no, will you make sure to use it? I'm Chrome by the way." Handing me a slip of paper he already had filled out while I was in the store, so sure of himself, I didn't hesitate to take it.
"Chrome huh? And is that your real name or just what your friends call you?" Not promising to use his number but instead to have him anticipating by his

phone for my call was just my way of taking back control of this hold he seem to have over me.

"No, Chrome is just for you." Damn, I thought, he got me, I'm done, I had to laugh at my own self for getting caught up now, when I look back at what I could have walked away from.

"Girl is you done yet?" Kat leaned over to my side of the Jeep and yelped out the window. I know she saw dude trying to holla at me, but sometimes Kat couldn't stand for a guy to step to me, she wasn't jealous or anything like that, she just felt the need to protect me as if I was her little sister, even though we were the same age, she was just a couple of months older than me.

"Kat, give me a minute here I'm talking and you're embarrassing me." I looked at her and tilted my head towards Chrome, hinting to her to chill for a minute.

"Fine, just don't take all night I'm trying to get to the club tonight not help it close, ya feel me?" She insisted on making Chrome feel real uncomfortable.

"So are you going to a club tonight? Which club was that?" He asked in a sly way pushing more conversation between us.

"All Stars, and then Casanova's with my girl here. Why? Are you trying to go with us?" I cunningly asked, hoping that he would.

"I don't know yet, maybe. I got some business to take care of, but if all goes well maybe we could link up later. Otherwise you have my number just call me." He said walking backwards heading for his car.

"Business? This late? What kind of work do you do that have you on call at this time of night?" My questioning was understandable due to the circumstances however it wouldn't hurt to know his finances status without having to ask him exactly how much money do you make?

"Well, let's just say it's more like a meeting. Yeah a late night meeting between me and another colleague." He was so smooth with his response, that, at that moment I still hadn't put two and two together.   All of his enigmatic skeletons would soon come later.

"Can we go now or are you waiting for him to drive around the block to come back here?"
I shook my head and laughed as I got in the car and reversed out of the gas station heading for a night of fun with Kat by my side, my ride or die Bitch.

CHAPTER 2 TWICE IN ONE NIGHT

All Stars was jumping that night, tourists, movie stars, Basketball players, and even some Hip Hop artists was there. It was always like that in Miami night life, and yet I was so out of place. Usually that was my scene too, being with Tony, he worked at a lot of happening party's and clubs, we always had a good time, but that night was different, it was the first night I would be at a club without him.

"I'm sorry Brook, I could see that this is too much for you right now. Tell you what, let's just head over to Casanova's and mellow out to Jazz music and sip on some Cognac." For once I didn't feel the need to argue with Kat on that, I could use a quiet scene tonight and still be out for her. I nodded my head and once again we were on the road. Casanova's was in Coconut Grove, it is a sexy Jazz club that even had poetry nights during the week, which I use to go to all the time back in the days before I was in my twenties. It started raining as soon as we pulled up to valet parking, thank God for valet, because I did not feel like running in the rain with these heels.

"Hello ladies, looking mighty good tonight, can I get you a table?" Carl, the host of the club was always so nice to us, but I just think he was happy for the eye candy.

"VIP's CARRRL, and you already know this because you stuck it in my garter belt at Shaye's the other night, remember? When I gave you that private lap dance and you didn't have no money on you?"

Kat wasted no time shoving the two VIP passes in his face, letting all his business hang out in front of the bouncers, as she walked passed him not even waiting for his reply. I strolled behind her and turn back to see Carl waving his hand to his waitresses to send over a bottle of Martel VSOP and two shot glasses, he didn't want Kat being any more obvious then she was already. I must say I felt like royalty that night, all the men were turning their heads, watching our perfect voluptuous shape body's and swaying hips as we walked by them.

Once we were seated Kat opened the bottle of brandy and pour two shots, one for me and for her, and we took it to the head at the same time, she refilled both of our glasses and at that moment the Base and the Saxophone players started to play soothing mellow notes, I sat back and consume the whole vibe of soft lights, and great music.

"Excuse me ladies but that gentleman over there in the white suite said to send this bottle of Hennessy Paradis over to you." Carl laid a very rare bottle of Hennessy, a very expensive bottle, my dad had a thing for fine Cognac that's how I recognize this bottle, it was one he admired the complex of the aroma and taste. I don't care how much it cost big ballers in Miami think they can have whatever they want with a bottle of expensive liquor,

both Kat and I was not falling for it, but we were
impressed by the gesture, or at least she was over
whelmed, by the way she marveled the liquor.

"Who you said sent it?" She asked Carl.
"Who cares who sent it Kat, remember we don't
go for that bull shit." I try to snap her out of it,
reminding her that it probably was game.

"And what's wrong with that? Did you see how
much this bottle is? It was on the top shelf of the bar,
girl ain't nuthin wrong we just saying thank you now
is that ok with you?" Kat try to convince me what
she seem to already convince herself, so I sat back
and shrug my shoulders as to say whatever.

"It is that guy across the floor in the other VIP
section. Do you want me to tell him to come over?"
Carl asked as if he needed too, Kat eyes was fill
with Christmas, the guy could be Jack the Ripper and
she would want to meet him.

"Yes, yes, tell him to come over and chill with
us."
She demanded to Carl as if he was her very own
personal butler. I had nothing to say, she was a wild
child and sometimes one just need to let her be. I
didn't hesitate to taste the cognac from the snifter
glass she poured for me, knowing that eventually I
would want a glass. Still, I was not interested in
meeting-

"Well, we meet again, second time for tonight."
No, it couldn't be, it was, Chrome! I could feel my

frown turning into a blushing smile instantly as I
looked up and saw those hypnotic eyes once again.

"When I told you where we were going tonight, I
really didn't think you were going to try to find me."
I softly said to him taking for granted that's why he is
here, moving over on the couch inviting Chrome to sit
with us. Kat was appreciative at the steps Chrome
took to get with me, as she gave him an approving
glass up to the sky.

"To be honest, I was going to be here tonight
anyway, but I never caught your name, and how rude
of me not to even ask." He was being a perfect
gentleman and I was enjoying being sort of say
'courted' if you will.

"Don't really remember dropping my name for you
to catch it, but seeing that you went to great extremes
such as buying this amazing bottle of Rare Hennessy
for me and my girl, guess you deserve a gift back. I'm
Brooklynn Haven, some of my friends call me
Brook." Enticing him with my small talk went well
with our surroundings.

"I'm impressed, you know your liquor, however it
wasn't too extreme seeing that it was my bottle to
begin with. I was just waiting for the right time and
person to share it with."
He said as he licked his smooth brown lips staring at
me with those light brown hazel eyes, making me feel
like no one else in the club matter at all to him but
me.

"Your bottle? Why do you have your own liquor here, I mean do they allow people to bring their own bottle?" I asked, curiously, but I guess maybe since he was in VIP.

"No Brook, Chrome is the owner of Casanova's sorry girl, I aaaint put two and two together when we ssaw him earlier." Kat words were starting to slur and her hand became heavy as she was waving her glass around talking to me.

"Owner, oh, but wait I thought Carl was the owner?"

I asked more clueless than ever now, because I don't remember ever seeing Chrome here before, his eyes are not one to forget.

"Nah, Carl is just my host, he runs the club for me, but I'm the banker behind it."
"So your meeting was here tonight at the club then?"
"Not exactly, but never mind that, when can we get to know each other a little more Brooklynn?" My name seems to roll off his tongue so lustfully.
"I thought that is what we were doing right now?" Playing back with his emotions was the center of my conversation with him.

"Well I was thinking more of just me and you, a table for two, no one else around getting to know each other." He was saying all the write words, but I was hesitant to be alone with him right now.

"Urgghh, I think I'm going to be sick."

Kat started to rub her head leaning it back on the sofa.

"Oh honey, I'm sorry. I think it's time for us to go. You don't look so hot." I said trying to hold her up and grabbing her little purses.

"Here let me give you a hand there, we can leave through the back door." Chrome said relieving Kat off of my arm onto his, and I was grateful that he came to the rescue of a damsel in distress. When we got to my Jeep, he help me put her in the back seat so she could lay out, and then he walked me over to my side and open the door for me.

"Thank you." I said to him getting in my seat.
"I would still like to continue getting to know you B. Tell you what, I'll pick you up tomorrow around one o'clock and we will go out for lunch, my treat."

He said licking his lips once again gazing at me with his seductive eyes.
"I guess if I say no, it wouldn't matter, you're still going to show up at my hotel room right?"
"If you say no, I'll respect that, I won't show up at your door, but I will ask again the next day, and maybe until you say yes, how will we get to know each other better unless you give us a chance?"
He requested for my time, I couldn't say no, even if I wanted to.

"Tomorrow is fine. I'll txt u where I'm staying at." and with that I close my door, and drove away, leaving him standing there with his hands join together in front of him looking like a real G.

The sound of Kat puking her guts out in the bathroom the next morning woke me up. Grabbing my cell phone off of the night table, I glanced at the time, still trying to focus, guess I was a little buzz still from last night because it took me awhile to see the time which was ten a.m. I jumped out of bed and ran into the bathroom, and immediately ran back out from the stench of Kats upset stomach.

"Oh my gosh what happen girl, did you die and come back? Is there any air fresheners here?" I said holding my hands over my mouth and nose, trying to keep from vomiting along with her.

"Uhhh, I have some incense in my bag over by the window, burn dat shit and call me up some pepto-bismol and maybe a cute nurse too." She said sitting on the floor by the toilet leaning up on the wall. Kat always loved the smell of incense and got me into them too, but she carried it around like someone carried their condoms.

"Now Kat, you know the best way to get over a hangover is to take a drink, so, here take this shot, and go lay back in bed cuz I need the bathroom. I'm soo running late." I handed her the shot glass which she unwillingly took, but knew that is exactly what she needed

"Where are you taking your trifling ass, while I'm here sick in bed in need of intensive care from you?" Slowly shuffling to her side of the bed she plopped down and asked me while watching me run around

the room trying to get ready for my date with
Chrome.

"Uh, you know that guy we met last night, the
owner of the Jazz club, well he is picking me up
around one for lunch, and that's it. I'm just going to
lunch with a nice guy." That was me trying to get out
of a confrontation with her, because I just know her
protective instincts will take over any minute, 1, 2, 3,

"Who are you trying to convince Brook? It's only
me and you. I heard all about this dude Chrome, he
ain't no Tony that's for sure, he ain't no joke
either. I don't know Brook, he got a lot of stacks but
he is known for being in the business if you get what I
mean."

In the midst of hustling around I stopped dead in my
tracks when she said 'in the business', we all know
that meant a drug dealer, contract killer.

"How do you know this?"
I was seriously rethinking my plans with him
today. I always had one rule, never date or mess with
a dealer, just wasn't my style, sure my Dad was a
contract killer back in his days before he met my
Mother, but he said he left that all behind when he
found out she was pregnant with me. Of course I
remember little things growing up, like Daddy taking
me out to Dairy Queen for ice cream one day and a
guy in a tannish brown eighty eight Oldsmobile
Cutlass Supreme pulled up and handed my Dad an
envelope filled with stacks and a key. I never knew
what it was for, but I knew I didn't like the way that
dude looked at me. There were other times, none I
care to think about right now.

"Well you know Carl comes to the strip a lot, and he always telling me stories about what Chrome does thinking I will get turned on because he hangs out with thugs."

"What I'm going to do? I can't go out with him. He is so damn fine though."

"Girl, aint nuthin wrong with one date, go and get you some, so you could at least get Tony out of your system then maybe we can get you a place and out of this depressing room." Kat said urging me to go. I shook my head, and said to myself one date, just one, and then I'll tell him that I am not interested in another date right now.

"While you are on your date, I think I'll call up one of my hoes to come and rehabilitate me."

She was sick, yet still horny, no figure.

"Just make sure your hoe doesn't walk off with any of my stuff, I'm not in the mood to cut a bitch tonight." I laid down house rules with Kat because pussy can easily distract her.

"Girl I got you, all yo shit is in here, so I will just get the room next door, because you know I need room to do my thang." I walked in the bathroom shutting the door behind me to ignore all of Kat's sexual escapade stories.

After my shower, I took my time getting ready, no longer in a rush to see Chrome, I was losing interest in him the more I thought about his lifestyle. Didn't feel like getting all dressed up anymore, instead I put on my tight fitted jeans that hugged my ass, and my black silk shirt and tucked it in my pants, instead of heels I threw on my black Coach sneakers. I looked like I was going out with friends not on a date with a hot gut, but that was my plan to make him lose interest in me. As I was pulling my curly red hair in a ponytail and curled my bang the hotel room phone rang.

"Hello, yes this is she. Oh fo real, ok I'll be right down." Kat hung up the phone, and I looked at her.

"Oh, that call was for you, it seems Mr. Baller didn't come to pick you up, nope, he sent a white stretched Limo for you, and it is waiting downstairs."

She said calmly, but I knew her better.
Both of us headed to the balcony running like we were little gits excited to check out the Limo.

"Hmm, he making sure the panties comes off tonight!"
"Whatever, do you see what I got on, this is not even worthy of sitting in a Limo like that, aint no panties coming off tonight."
"Oh pahlease, even in your play clothes your light coffee complexion ass is still calling to be touched and I can see your nipples through your plain black silk shirt, and if he has you in air condition your shit is going to be hard, looking like rock candy to his ass You aint fooling no one but yourself."
She had a way of words when she talked about a woman's anatomy, but I wasn't changing, and I blew

a kiss to her as I walked out the door while she sat on the balcony watching in envy.

CHAPTER 3 OVER SEAS

"Are you Miss. Brooklyn?"
The Driver of the Limo asked, he was tall dark and handsome.

"Yes I am, and where is Mr. Chrome?"
I asked looking in the limo noticing no one was in there.

"He will be meeting you at the boat dock."
"Boat Dock? He didn't say anything about boat dock."
"I'm sorry Ma'am he just said to bring you there to meet him." There was no point in asking the Driver anything else, it seems that Chrome had his plans, and only he knew what they were. I got in the limo, this big stretched limo just for little ol' me. There was a bottle of Crystal in a bucket of ice and a glass with a strawberry placed on the rim, what could it hurt? I downed about three glasses of champagne before we arrived at Biscayne Bay Boat Dock. Chrome was standing in the same position I left him in last night, only this time he was wearing a grey suit with a purple pin stripe shirt and dark purple tie to match now I felt under dress and so stupid. The Driver opened up the door, and put his hand out to help me out of the limo.

I walked up to Chrome who was patiently waiting for me.

"I'm sorry I didn't know we were supposed to dress up, you said only lunch."

I apologized to him, seeing that he went out his way to make a good impression.

"You have nothing to be sorry about, you look very beautiful, and I am honored to have you in my presence for lunch."

For a thug he sure didn't talk or act like one, he sounded very educated and smooth, not rough and improper. Standing next to him I figure he was about six feet tall, because I am five feet six inches without heels. It was very securing to stand next to him and look in his gorgeous eyes.

"So where exactly are we eating lunch, is it on one of these boats or here near the dock?" I asked looking around to see what was near.

"We are not having lunch here or on the boat, but we are taking a boat ride to lunch." He was full of surprises today. He smiled at me, took my hand and I followed him onto this breath taking yacht.

"This is our Captain for the day, and my boy Six Two. We go way back, I don't make a move without him. Six Two, this is B, short for Brooklynn, and she's feisty so be careful what you say to her." Chrome introduced me to Six Two, and he was just that, six feet two inches tall dark skin tone with dreads down his back and muscle top body, and I just love how Chrome gave me a nickname.

"It is a pleasure to finally meet the lady that has been taking over all our conversation lately, Chance has nonstop talking about you so much I feel like I already know you."

Six Two said, revealing Chrome's real name taking my hand and kissing the back of it.

"Wow, well it's nice to meet you to, and Chance is that your real name Chrome?"
 I replied with a smile.

"Well if you will excuse me, I'll get us going to our destination." He said, making his exit, so Chrome and I could be alone.

"So are you going to tell me about your name and where we are going?" I asked him, knowing he will just evade my curiosity.

"Ok it's only fair, my real name is Chance Rome, and why would I ruin the surprise by telling you where we're going? Good things come to those who wait. Besides I have something for you."

He was just full of surprises today, and I was intrigue by it all, but still needed to not allow myself to fall too hard for him. I followed him below deck without another word. Even though this guy was pulling out all the stops for me, I couldn't help but to think about when Tony use to do so many romantic things for me, plan romantic vacations on weekends, I miss all of that, but he mess that up, not me. The whole time I was with Tony, never did I tip toe out the door on him, this is my first date with someone else in six years.

"Here, this is for you, just a little something for this afternoon, and maybe later."

Chrome handed me a big white box with a yellow ribbon. This is too much I thought to myself, he barely knows me, yet he is spending so much money on me. I'm not a gold digger, and never ask for all of this, he could have taken me to Miami Subs for wings, and I would have been happy with that, or even ordered in Chinese food. I didn't want to seem ungrateful for his efforts, so I took the box with a gracious smile. In it, was an elegant white satin dress, low cut in the front and back with a diamond closure at the front and a crystal choker to finish it off, I was speechless, of course there was a pair of clear glass heels with it.

"This is gorgeous Chrome, but I can't really accept this. It's too much." I laid the dress back in the box.

"This is why I'm so drawn into you, you are not like other women, and they would have jumped to take that dress in a second. I hope I haven't offended you, but honestly I just saw this dress and thought how beautiful you would look in it."
He was really trying to be a perfect date, I picked up the dress and pressed it against my body, it was really exquisite.

"Well, can I get some privacy to change in this lovely dress?" I asked him.

"Oh, of course, my bad, I'll be on deck if you need anything." He closed the door behind him, and I was left alone to get dress. I took my hair out of the simple pony tail, and let my deep red locks hang down, my hair was not that long but it is thick and full just a little bit past my shoulders. I slipped on the dress, and felt it fall into place gripping on to my curvaceous figure, it felt like satin sheets, smooth and silky. There was a vanity table in the room, filled with different kinds of make-up and lipsticks, this is different for a guy to think of every detail a women would need to get ready, I thought to myself. Burgundy wine color lipstick went well with my light brown cinnamon complexion. The glass heels were a perfect fit, and looked good with the dress. I glanced at myself one more time in front of the mirror before walking out the door to meet with my charming date.

Chrome gasped at how amazing I looked, it made me blush all over, even though I have dresses like this.

"You are a vision of beauty I am a luck guy today." Chrome whispered in my ears holding me close to him. We stood on the side of the Yacht and I gazed at the open ocean before us, this moment was the most romantic moment I have had in a very long time, I couldn't help but wondered though, if Tony was laid up with that hoe, or some next bitch already. Chrome stood behind me with his arms wrapped around my little waist, I could smell his expensive Burberry cologne, and it was nice on him.

"You see the ocean out there in the horizon you are worth all that and then some." He continued to whisper in my ear, giving me goose bumps as I felt the slight touch of his lips when he talked.

"So you just know all the right things to say to get a woman to fall all over you huh?" I asked trying to figure out if this was his game, or real.

"Nah, B, from the moment I met you, it was plain to see you were no hood rat chick, or even some naive girl that just fall for any dude that paid her attention. You got that classy lady look and presence about you, and I am just giving you what you deserve. The world, even if it's only lunch."

He had all the right words, and moves, I couldn't walk away just yet. Maybe his business is his business, and I could allow myself with him for right now. "Well even though all of this is breath taking, I'm starving now, I just can't wait to see what you have for us to eat, just hope it aint no fruits and veggies cuz a girl need some meat, if you know what I mean." I said to him flirting at the same time.

"Oh, well we mean to take care of that right... about.....now." As soon as he said now, a small Island, all lighted up like Christmas Eve popped up in the short distance, the closer we came to it the bigger it got, I can see a big white tent with bright lights hanging from the out lay of it, and there also seemed to be a cabin of some sort on the Island, was this a resort or something?

"C'mon, B, we are here." He took my hand in his and we walked down the stairs onto a small Pier leading to the private beach area. When we got to the sand, he bent down and slipped off my glass heels, and held it in his hands as we continued to walk over to the tent.

"An ol' friend of mine, own this private resort here in the Bahamas, he owed me a favor, so I thought now was a perfect time to collect on it."

Chrome eyes looked pleased to see everything seem to fall in place as he talked.

"Woww, this is really nice." I said holding on to his arm. We walked in the tent where a Waiter was waiting with a bucket of ice and a bottle of Champagne. In the middle of the tent was a table with two chairs and some rose petals all around it. My mind was blown away.

"This is just lunch?" I asked sarcastically but still impressed by it all.

"Actually no, this is where we are having lunch, here have a seat and I will show you just what lunch is." In a cocky attempt he said pulling out a chair for me to sit, and then as he sat the Waiter came over and pours Champagne into both of our glasses. I couldn't wait to drink it, I needed it to calm my nerves, never had I been so nervous before. The Waiter places a dish on the table and uncovered it. There was some sort of roast or chicken as the main dish covered in a red sauce with pineapples around it. I had no idea what this could be.

"It is called peeking duck, it's one of my favorite dishes." Chrome said to me, as he notice the uncertainty look on my face when the Waiter took off the lid.

"I don't think I ever had duck before." I said slowly taking a gulp in fear of having to eat a duck, even though it smelled damn good and sweet, just the thought of it being a duck was not appealing to me.

"Here, let me show you how to eat it."

He said bringing his chair around to the side of the table sitting closer to me. He grabbed a pair of chop sticks and picked up a piece of the duck dipped it into a sauce and placed it in my mouth, even though I was reluctant to even try it, just thought I would since he was catering to me. The duck was delicious, it was sweet and tangy at the same time, I don't know if it was the duck or the way Chrome fed it to me, but that moment was orgasmic.

"Well?" He asked, but I'm sure he knew the answer from my expression on my face of enjoyment.

"Well, it is mouthwatering, and I can't help but want to taste some more." I flirtatiously said to him.

"That is not a problem at all, but I have something else I want you to taste." He whispered to me as he signaled for the waiter to bring out another dish, what could this be? I thought feeling like a kid on

Christmas morning getting ready to open her gifts. The waiter brought the dish out and uncovers what looked like it could be Jelly fish from its translucent appearance. Shaking my head thinking I am not eating Jelly fish.

"This is a delicacy, and it intrigues me, because if not cooked right it can kill you, it's called Fugu s Sashimi it's a blow fish." So now he wants me to eat something that can actually kill people....Nice I thought.

"I am trusting you here, but just so you know, my girl Kat knows where I am and if I don't return you will be looking over your shoulder every day."

I taunted him a little since he was making me try all this weird shit. Maybe he watched too much Andrew Zimmerman shows. However I tasted it and it didn't have much flavor to it until he fed me another piece that was dipped in a special sauce. It was alright, however I wouldn't order it again.

After lunch, I decided to call and check on Kat, just in case I make it back late. Chrome went to check on the rest of his plans for us, and I had time to make a call to her.

"Umm, hello, ohhh, who dis?" Kat answered the phone, and by the way she sounded, I figure she was not alone.

"Kat, it's me, I'm just checking in girl."

"Brook, oh hold baby I gotta take this call, yeah why don't you go get that. Hey Brook girl, how is everything going?"

Kat was very much entangled with a hook up.

"I'm good, everything is going good, I just wanted to check on you and if you were feeling better, but I can see that you are being well taken care of." I laugh at the thought of us both being taken care of tonight.

"Oh you know me already, I got to have my nurse to help me sweat this hangover off, but anyway, how is dude treating you?"

"He has been all too real, and I love it, which makes this hard for me to walk away from him, but I will be back late so don't wait up." I cut our conversation short when Chrome headed back to me.

"Are you ready beautiful to see what else I have in store for us tonight?"

Chrome put his hand out for me to join him once again, and with no worries that he would do me wrong I went with him. He lured me into the cabin on the beach, when I went inside there was a fireplace already lit up, a king size bed with satin sheets, and a heart shape Jacuzzi on the deck outside.

"Well here we are, and please don't think I brought you here to just have sex with you, I just got the feeling that you were stressed out last night at the

club, so this is my way of giving you a relaxing,
pampering evening."

Chrome was right I really could use some pampering,
even if it was by another man.

    "This is exactly what I need, but I don't even have
a bathing suit, or were you planning on me getting
into the Jacuzzi naked?"

I taunted him with sexual hints, because let's be real,
he was fine as hell, and Tony fucked up with me not
the other way around, why shouldn't I have my cake
and eat it too.

    "Well, I can't say the thought didn't enter my
mind, but naw B there is a bathing suit and robe
waiting for you in the bathroom, so please make
yourself comfortable and I'll meet you in the
Jacuzzi." He swayed me with his words. This had to
be a dream, he couldn't be real, I kept telling
myself. In the bathroom which, by the way, had a
shower and a whirl pool tub, there was a two piece
bikini bathing suit, and it fit me perfect. I opened the
sliding door that led to the deck with the Jacuzzi, it
was already bubbling but Chrome wasn't there yet. I
slowly got in and rested my head back to the
massaging stream of water, and I closed my
eyes. Enjoying myself too much, Chrome came out
and landed a strawberry in my mouth.

    "Mmm, that's sweet." I said to him
complimenting on more than the strawberry.

"I'm sure it is not as sweet as you. B, you mind if I ask you a question?" He could ask me anything he wanted at that point.

"No, I don't mind, what's up?"
"How is it that a woman like you don't have a man keeping her home at night so another man like myself can get a hold of her at a club. I mean if you was my woman, and I hope you will be, I would know your every move, and another man wouldn't even be an issue." He came out of nowhere with that, and I really didn't know what to make of it.

"I really don't want to go into details, but I did have a good man once, for a long time, but I guess I wasn't good enough, because he had other agendas." Thinking about Tony was not what I wanted to do right now, I needed to vent and relax my mind right now, don't even know what to say to my boss about my abrupt absences from work for the past two days. I loved my job at the bank I have worked there for about three years, and was on my way for a big promotion handling big business loans and investments, which would mean no more being just a teller.

"Naw, never dat, you are more than good enough, he just didn't know what he had. It's like these little niggas I fuck wit on these streets every day, trying to teach them to appreciate what they have and don't shit it away." Chrome said moving closer to me, he was feeling me on a different level now that I have open up a little to him, but now it was my turn to get his story.

"Tell me something now, and I hope this doesn't come out to blunt, but I need to know, are you in the drug game?" I almost choked just asking him, not really wanting an answer.

"Yeah, that is being blunt, I won't hold it against you though." He said with a smile, trying to divert from answering, but when he saw the look that I gave him, letting him know we weren't going any further until I got my answers, he leaned back and said,

"Drug game is not what I would call it, let's just say I do my business in the streets, with niggas I trust, and I keep it moving, and it's personal to me." He answered but didn't, guess if I was a cop, there is nothing I could hold him on, and maybe that is what he intended.

"Enough talk." He whispered to me moving in for a kiss. I didn't hesitate kissing him, even though I said I wouldn't get involved with a dealer, this time I would look pass that, because I was with a straight and narrow, he did me wrong, now I'm with a straight G and I wanted to give him all my goodies tonight.

His kiss was inviting and luring, passionately tonging me down, he was licking and sucking my neck which was sending my emotions wild. I straddle him in the hot tub, kissing him back, lacing my lips on his neck and muscular chest. I couldn't help but stare into his eyes while making out with him, they were so damn sexy and dreamy looking, drawing me in for a sexual rise. Chromes hands were sensitive and electric to the touch at the same time, making me have goose bumps, they completely uncover me and his exploration of my body with his mouth began. Tasting, licking, sucking, touching my body in all the vital points, driving me wild, causing my sweet hairless peach to get gushy and wet, too bad we were in the Jacuzzi, otherwise it would have been easier for him to tell my body was pleased with what he was doing to me.

"Let's take this inside, I could show you such pleasure out of the tub." Chrome picked me up and took me inside the cabin, he laid me down on a shagged rug in front of the fire place, standing over me with his swole manhood, picked up a bottle of champagne and poured it on me, from my breast on down. He got on his knees, and started to slurp up the champagne, sucking my tight aroused nipples, slowly moving down to my precious peach. By the way Chrome picked up my legs, laying my juicy peach in his mouth instantly enduring all my vibrant juices to flow like a raging river out of me, he meant to please me only, he wasn't expecting anything back, but I didn't want to receive and not give. I took him by surprise when in return, I laid him down by pushing his shoulders, pinning him into the floor, kissing his lips, his neck, his stomach, but before I could lay my full lips around his brick of thickness, he grabbed my arms and pulled me back up,

"Today is for you, later you make it about me." He calmly said pulling me in for another kiss, positioning me on his swole chocolate shaft. Riding him up and dropping my plump ass down, curving around his manhood made for the perfect orgasm that lead to my body trembling afterwards laying on him catching one after another not wanting to lose this feeling, because it's just what I needed. I fell asleep in his arms that night.

"What are you thinking about?" I asked him, waking up right beside him to see that he was already up and deep in thought.

"Hey you, I didn't mean to wake you up, I was just laying here wondering how I ended up with such a beautiful Lady." He said, being a little too full of shit. The way he was staring at the ceiling a moment ago, it seemed like the world was on his shoulders, however, this night we spent together was not getting ruined by my intrusion into his hustle life.

"You need to wonder how to keep a beautiful Lady like me." I said back to him smiling, but little did he know I was ready for him to keep me. Guess life is like that sometimes, you spend so much time trying to be with the right guy that you miss out on the perfect ones, so I wasn't taking no chances, I'm jumping on this wagon and riding it till the wheels fall off.

"I'm working on that right now as we speak."

He lowered his voice and licked his lips as he went under the sheets and gave me such pleasures over again.

Later that day I packed up all of the stuff he gave me in a Lou Vuitton suitcase he also provided me with, that had perfume gift sets and a few Jazz cd's in it, guess he was more into Jazz than just his club. We headed back to the Yacht to go home. "So where is the gorgeous house that my Lady lives in, so that I can take her home and hope to get invited in?"

"I stay at the Hotel right now. I haven't really got a chance to look for my own place yet." I was so caught up with hanging out with Chrome, that not only have I missed a few days of work, I also had not look for a place to live, without Tony.

"We can't have that now. How about we go get your things and you and I spend the rest of the day looking for the right pad for you?"

"What about your busy schedule? And besides, my girl Kat is still with me at the Hotel."
"We can bring her along, if you want." He said, escorting me off the Yacht and to the Limo that was patiently waiting for us.

When we arrived at the Hotel, I went up to my room by myself leaving Chrome to wait in the car. I anxiously opened up my room door to find that Kat had not returned from her night out with her playmate, but I didn't want to keep Chrome waiting, so I packed up all of my stuff, and left Kat a letter and some money to cover the room cost, and told her as soon as I get settled in a place, I would send her the address. When I got in the elevator, I took a deep breath, and exhale, not wanting to be too obvious to Chrome.

"Here let me take that for you." He said, approaching me and taking my suitcases off of the trolley I had them on and loading them in the limo.

"I also took the liberty to have Six Two bring your ride to my house until we find you a place, then he will deliver your Jeep to you, I hope that was ok?"

"Yeah, that's cool, I guess."

Chrome had a realtor meet us at the first spot, it was a big three bedroom house in Cottage Grove, but I was not digging it, too much for just me and to close to Tony. I liked big places, but if it was just for me, a two bedroom in the city would fit me nice.

"If this is not what you looking for, tell me what would be your dream home?" The realtor asked both Chrome and I, guess she got the idea that we were married, or looking for a place for both of us, but to be honest, I just got out of living with a guy, I was not ready to be living under the same roof with another, especially not one I just met.

"I just would like a small two bedroom, nothing to fancy, but def, want a big kitchen, and gotta have a nice master bathroom, and preferably in the city."

Hope I was asking for the impossible at short notice.

"What do you have in my area like that?" Chrome asked her, and confused me. I would think a big shot like him would have his crib somewhere out of the city, secluded from everybody in the dope game.

"You live in the City, how come?" I asked him back in the limo following the realtor to the next showing.

"I was born in Dade County, raised in Liberty City with all my fam and Dawgs, so it's only right that sleep where I play all day, and see firsthand what's going down in my own hood. I should be asking you, why would you bring your pretty ass to live in here, I would think you would prefer somewhere upscale?"

He teasingly asked me, and by the way he smiled I could tell he was happy that I would be even more close to him than he thought. Driving through Liberty city, and seeing the poverty level of the whole neighborhood would seem depressing to an outsider, however, I found comfort in it right now, I would get no judgments, or dirty looks from anyone because of my status with Tony, but instead open arms and laughter of the kids playing on the deteriated playground that has been left behind for them.

"No, here is perfect for me, I don't care to live in some snobby neighborhood that's boring."

I said back smiling at Chrome. We pulled up to the end of the street, with a long driveway that lead to a yellow house, with a broken old wire gate around it, but yet it was beautiful, it was simple, and yet screamed for attention, love and care. When we went inside, the living room was right in the front, and the two bedrooms were on either side of the house, the master bedroom was nice and big, with a huge closet, I smiled from ear to ear, the kitchen was big too with an eat in nook, and then by my surprise, the backyard was filled with trees and nice landscape, someone loved to plant trees.

"I love it, I'll take it. How much is the owner looking for?" I asked the realtor, ready to pay asking price for it. The realtor looked at Chrome first before she gave me an answer, which didn't sit right with me.

"Well, this is actually a foreclosed home, and the bank is just asking for a hundred fifty thousand give or take." The realtor answered and still looking at Chrome for approval, and he nodded his head, what the hell was that? Did he own the house or something?

"Chrome, can I talk to you for a moment, alone?" I said to him, pulling his hand to step out of the room for privacy.

"What's going on? Why is she looking at you, when I am the one buying the house?" I just couldn't understand what the whole idea was.

"It's nothing everybody around here just shows respect that's all." He sounded so much like a mob boss, and I wanted to just walk out of there, but it was too late.

"Well the house is yours, if you want to go ahead and sign the papers. I'll give you the keys and handle everything for you myself."

She said, already having the paper work ready for me to sign and own the house, and just like that the house was mine, and no sooner did she hand me the keys, did Chrome got on his phone and called for a cleanup crew, and alarm company to secure my house.

"Listen B, I would love to stay tonight and help you move in, but I got a urgent meeting to attend to, Six Two will bring your ride, and I'll have an interior decorator come by and help you furnish the house, my house warming gift for you. If you need anything else just hit me up and I will be here as soon as I can."

By the way Chrome moved, it was if he made me his laid up woman already, and I can't help but to except it, at least for now.

"Alright, guess I'll see you later, and thanks for everything again." I kissed him on the cheek, and he left. No sooner then he left I got a phone call from Kat.

"Hello."
"Thanks for leaving me chic, where are you now anyway?" Kat sounded a bit angry.
"I didn't leave you on purpose. Didn't you get my letter I left you?"
"A sticky note, that's what you call a letter, ha ha I'm clowin, it's cool, I know you would never leave me hanging, I just wanted to bust your balls. So did you find a place yet, and going house hunting with Chrome, that's kind of fast isn't it?" Kat did not hesitate getting my blood pumping.

"You are so crazy Kat, you lucky I love you, and yes I found a place, and Chrome being with me is not that serious, he just had a hook up that's all. Anyway, I'm texting you the address right now, so get your butt over here right now, cuz some decorator is coming over and I don't want to do this alone."

I was really nervous about this interior decorator that Chrome had coming over, and didn't know much about decorating except gettin a couch and table to match.

"Girl have no fear Kat's on her way, I'll stop and bring some wings and beer." Kat was so silly, and she love to bring food for any occasion, and it always included wings and beer.

CHAPTER 4 THE UNVEILING

Kat and I spent the afternoon with the Interior Decorator Shelia, and she knew her stuff. By the end of the day, she had the whole house with a scheme that I would love. Dark shades of Grey for the walls, beautiful stainless steel and black appliances for the kitchen, not to mention marble counters, deep red sleek sofa, and the master bedroom, I ordered a queen size bed with a canopy, and black laced curtains. By the end of the week my house would be ready, as for tonight, it was just me and Kat with wings, and beer, on the floor of the living room chilling like old times.

"So are you going to work tomorrow?" Kat asked as we laid on a blow up mattress we got out of Target, rubbing our full stomachs.

"I have to girl, otherwise who's going to pay these bills I'm about to have. I hope boss man ain't mad at me." I complained to Kat.
"Girl, just let me come in with you, and I'll make him forget that you even took a leave of absence." Kat used her body skills to get things she needed and wanted, but I would never use her like that, she was my girl, and that would be abusing our friendship.

"It's ok Kat, I made a call to Vikki earlier about my days off, and told her it was a family emergency that couldn't be helped, she said that she would handle boss man for me, but I would have to make an appearance tomorrow."

"Good, cuz the last thing you need is to be dancing with me in the clubs, with your wack ass booty shake I would end up having to apologize for you and let the customers know you was mentally ill for your ass to make one dollar."

Kat chuckled and snorted slapping me on the arm getting a kick out of her own jokes.

"Whatever, my booty shakes just fine, you just worried I might come and shut the whole club down with my zumba dance and put you out of work." It was my turn to chuckle and slap her on the arm with my snap back joke. With that we both laughed knowing I was full of shit, I don't know how to begin to shake my booty like Kat, I was more of a slow dancer.

The next day at work, I wore my grey pants suit black heels and my white blouse that sinuates my silhouette top frame of my body, didn't want to look to obvious just enough to distract boss man from firing his best employee that was on her way to a promotion. Unlocking the doors to the bank at eight thirty in the morning, I walked in and turned off the alarm. Only the boss man, Vikki and I had keys to the bank. Seeing that I was the first one there today gave me an advantage to get on boss man's good side, I started the coffee pot in his office, on my way to the bank I picked up a fresh package of Columbian coffee from this gourmet shop around the corner from our bank. We were located right smack of downtown

Miami, a big branch, and handled a lot of major commercial clients. After setting up coffee for our customers as well, I also laid out doughnuts, coffee crumb cakes, and napkins. Then the rest of my co-workers started to arrive one by one.

"Good Morning, good morning."

I greeted them as they walked in, and in the back ground I could see boss man pulling up in his new Maserati Granturismo sports car, that he got from a big major Pharmaceutical company account he landed last month.

"Well, hello Ms. Brooklyn, I see we are ready for work this morning I hope." He said to me, standing there in his Brooks Brothers (Madison Saxxon suit) I know my designers. He was good looking for an Italian man in his early forty's, his grey hair streaks mixed in with the dark black hairs gave away his age, but giving him the look of a distinguish gentleman as well.

"Good Morning Mr. Valentino, there is coffee ready in your office, and I took the liberty of making calls and appointments that I have missed this past week for today, so that I do not fall behind." My speech was well planned out, in hopes of regaining his trust in me and letting him know I can handle my job.

"That is great news. I have to tell you that I was worried that I would not have my shining star beside me when the time comes for that new promotion that is lingering in the air Ms. Brooklyn."

He laid his briefcase on his cherry wood desk, unbuttoning his blazer telling me he missed me in so many words.

"No, we couldn't have that sir." I said to him, putting both my hands on his desk leaning forward facing him to give him a glimpse of my body causing him to move his concentration on my breast instead of my eyes, taking control of my situation and getting back in charge.

"Well if that is all sir, I would like to get back to work, unless you have something else for me to do?" I said to him still leaning over his desk with heaving breasts.

"No, no, nothing um now, just that I am glad you are back." He barely got his words out, clearing his throat.

I handle work that day like I was already head supervisor of home loans at the bank, and was just about ready to work through lunch when Chrome walked in.

"This is a surprise." I said to him cautiously, hoping that no one in the bank would know him, or what he does.

"Just the banker I wanted to see. You look good, so how many dudes try to step to you today?" He asked me jokingly.

"Here, come to my desk so we could have more privacy." Grabbing him by the hand and walking over to my desk, I dared not to look up in fear of being stared at from everybody around, but when I sat down in my chair no one was even paying attention.

"You ok B? You look real nervous."
Chrome noticed I was on edged.

"You know what, I have just been working so much today that my nerves are getting the better of me."

"Hey, that is why I came, to ask my hard working lady to lunch." He said walking behind my desk and rubbing my shoulders.

"I wasn't going to take one today, but that sounds just like what I need." Grabbing my small black purse and keys I agreed to meet to meet Him out by his car while I let Vikki know I was taking my break. Really, I didn't want anybody from my job see me leaving with Chrome, everyone knew Tony and I wasn't ready to let my personal life in the work place be the latest gossip. Chrome took me to a quiet Cuban restaurant for lunch, he didn't know yet, but this was one of my favorite foods to eat. I ordered a shrimp cocktail and a Versailles salad, fresh mango, pecans and goat cheese, you can't go wrong.

"Sorry for popping up at your job like that, really all I wanted to do was to see you, I can't explain it but I feel my day is not complete without you in it."
Chrome was definitely wearing his heart on his sleeve, I thought thug niggas was hard and always

had a wall up when it came to a chick, but here was
this dude, showing me nothing but respect and
charm, he was throwing me off from my defense, it's
time I realize that Tony and I are over, and Chrome
is the guy to help me get back my heart.

"Wow, I wasn't expecting this, I don't even know
what to say, except, I kind of feel the same way too,
but I don't want to move to fast, space and time is
what I really need to heal. However I want you in my
life to help me with it."
I answered him holding his hands across the table.

"Whew, you don't know what you do to me, I got
all these feelings for you so quickly, but I learn to
trust my feelings a long time ago, but there is one
thing I need to show you before we can move on."
He said, giving off this mysterious feel to me.

"Ok, but it will have to be after work, I get off at
four."

"Meet me at this address when you get off, I'll be
waiting."
Chrome handed me a slip of paper with an address
on it, kissed me on my cheeks ever so gently and
drove off. I went back inside the bank, still in hopes
of no one noticing him with me, and got back to work.
Before leaving the parking lot after work to meet
Chrome, I called Kat to let her know I wouldn't be
home before she left for her job.

"Hey Brook money, what's up? I'm bout to get
ready for work." She answered her cell, whenever we

both were doing our thang getting money, she would always say money after my name.

"Hi Kat honey, I just called to let you know Chrome wants me to meet up with him somewhere, so I won't be home before you leave, but I'll see you later right?" I asked her to see if she was coming back, I loved my new place, but I hated being alone there.

"Fo sho Brook Baby, it will be after the club close tonight but I'll be back. Love you, and stay safe."

Kat said to me before we hung up. I know Chrome was waiting for me, but still I couldn't help but hesitate on the fact that maybe this wasn't a good idea, and I started the what if's questioning to myself, after minutes of should I go or not, I turned on the ignition and headed for the address, what the hell I thought, I already agreed to be his woman, might as well see what else I got myself into. Driving up to the address which was in the back cut of the open road, secluded from the rest of the world, had me thinking turn around now, leave, don't go any further, but what do I do. I parked my truck besides Chromes and texted him that I was outside, hell he needed to come meet me out here. I am not walking in by myself.

"Glad to see you made it B, for a moment there I thought I would have to send my Goons to look for you." He said laughing, but I wasn't finding that shit funny.
'Goons' was a thug term of Guys who were down for whatever ride or die homies.

"Goons? Whatever boy, why do you have me out here in this neck of the woods?" I asked him with one eyebrow up before I took another step in.

"Well if you come with me I will show you." He said reaching out for my hands and taking me into the building.

As soon as we walked in, there was a table full of guns, all different kinds, anything from a revolver to a machine gun, what the hell is all this for?

"What are we doing here Chrome?" I asked with anger in my voice, not understanding what the purpose of him bringing me here was.

"Calm down B, this is a gun range, my very own personal place that my boy P.A. here runs for me. I brought you here to show you how to protect yourself if it ever comes to that and I'm not around." He explained, holding my arm from me leaving out the door.

"Protect myself? Is all this really necessary? I'm not ready for this. I never had to protect myself from anything or anyone before, especially not with no gun." I said still hesitant.

"Will you do it for me then? It will put my mind to ease if I knew you could handle a gun. Please." He pleaded with me, staring at me with those dreamy eyes that pulled me in his world again.

"Fine, if it will make you FEEL better. Let's do this and get it over with."

I gave in throwing my purse and keys down on the table next to the first gun, which was a nine mm semi-automatic, it fitted nice in the palm of my hands.

"That fits you perfect. Let's get started."
He said to me with an approval smile, and I followed him to the back of what seems to be an old warehouse building. There were targets set up in the back, cans, dummies, and the ol time paper ones.

"First things First B, hold the gun away from your body, and with a good grip. Never ever pull the trigger, you have to squeeze it, and always remember to keep both eyes open so you can see and focus on your target." He said coming up close behind me, extending my arms straight forward, and placing his hands over mines on the gun aiming at a dummy body. I could feel his breath on my neck, and his heart beating against my back, he had nothing but a wife beater on and a pair of jeans, guess this was his workout clothes, a big difference from his suits. I focused on the target, and I listened to his voice as I squeezed the trigger and shot, 'Bang Bang Bang Bang'. I shot four times, it was nothing much to it, and then we walked up to the dummy to see how I did.

"Oh shit! Damn you sure you never did this before?" He asked me in disbelief, the dummy had two shots in the head, and two in the heart. I shook my head in denial, either I have done this before, or he was a good ass teacher. After that I tried a 357 magnum which had a stronger kick to it, a double barrel shotgun and of course the Mac Ten machine gun that sounded like a rail of bullets shooting and in the end the magnum was my favorite, and Chrome gave me it to have with ammunition and all. This was a crazy date to have, but I have to admit it was mad fun. The thought of why we were even here, and me walking out with a loaded weapon did not sit with me to well though, and it was plain out in the open exactly what I was getting myself into being with Chrome and his lifestyle, but I didn't intend to go in with my eyes closed.

CHAPTER 5 CAN'T STAND THE HEAT GET OUT THE KITCHEN

Between going back and forth from my place to Chrome's place was hectic, the one thing that Tony and I had was a stable place living together, eating together, just about everything together. Damn why did he have to go fuck that up, I was missing him a lot, even though Chrome was taking care of me and all my needs, but it just wasn't the same or enough.

Kat and I became roommates, she stayed in the guestroom rent free, I couldn't charge my girl, Chrome paid all my bills anyway, besides she kept me company on the nights she didn't have to work and Chrome was out on "business." What Chrome and I had was almost an understanding relationship, from my understanding he was faithful, loyal, took care any of my needs financially and physically, oh and when he lay it on me, I was down for the count, and he was always satisfied as well, he would say I have the juicy pussy that makes him thirsty for more. I guess when shit became real is when he started to have me more around him when he did his deals. He stopped excusing himself when the time would arise, instead he would have me sit next to him all dolled up matching his formal suit wear, and both of us drizzled in jewels and diamond stud earrings in his ears. Soon I became known as Chrome's Brooklynn, I would count the case of money when "Associates" would buy bricks of cocaine from him, and he would taste the merchandise when he was the buyer, knowing that I had my limits and that was no hard drugs for me, the only thing I did and never in the presence of Chrome was smoke weed with my girl Kat or home alone. However, he did teach me how to check the potency of the merchandise without having to taste it by testing it for quality with a chem stick, watching to see the level go up, the higher the better, anything below sixty percent he wasn't dealing with.

Chrome always gave me a cut out of his seventy five percent, after he paid his boys, it was saying that whatever he had, I had, and that was the one thing I adored him for. Don't get it twisted though your girl Brooklynn was no fool, remember Daddy schooled me, so when I had so much money stacking up, in fear of getting robbed or feds coming through the doors, I made plans with Kat to go on vacation to the Cayman Islands, without Chrome. He *thought* it was about girl time, we needing a little pampering, and he had no problem knowing his woman would be back with tanned ass. It's funny to me now, because we took a big risk stashing money into the banks overseas without me telling Chrome the real deal, but if push came to shove I wanted one secrete of my own, and I learned that from Tony, who held many secretes. As we got off the plane the whole experience was beautiful, I could only wish that we weren't there for business, it would have been very romantic to have Chrome here with me instead.

I had arranged for a limo to pick us up at the airport and transport us to our Hotel. No sooner then we got in the limo that Kat started pouring glasses of champagne and stuffing caviar with crackers down her hatchet, she was enjoying every minute of this trip, and I just hope she remembers what we are here for. Our hotel suite was nothing of the ordinary, a luxurious room with a deck right onto the beach, a fully loaded bar, and awaiting us was two big strawberry daiquiris, as if Kat needed more alcohol in her system.

"Now this is the life girl, I could get use to this real fast. We should just stay here and live."
Kat was taken by all the beautiful scenery and the drinks.

"Come on Kat you know we are here for business not pleasure. I really need you to stay focus with me here." I said sternly reminding her of what we came to do. Kat jumped to her feet from the comfortable soft lazy boy chair, put her drink down on the table, and threw her human quality weaved hair back into a ponytail, pulled out her reading glasses that transformed her from a nightingale beauty to a gorgeous educated looking woman.

"Let's do this Brook, I'm ready."
She said, assuring me that she has not forgotten. With a smile on my face I grabbed my briefcase filled up with stacks of one hundred dollar bills and headed to meet the prestige Manager of the bank I was depositing my money into. His name was Mikhail Roshnici, a close friend to my boss Mr. Valentino, so it was all a good hook up for me, but I couldn't shake this crazy notion that someone was following Kat and me. I kept looking over my shoulder everywhere we went that day, to the bank, then shopping with Kat and later to lunch then back to the resort, but when I

would turn my head there would be no one familiar, just the locals going about their business. Kat tried to reassure me that it was all in my head, because she didn't see anything suspicious either.

"Relax Brook baby, it's your nerves, you just feeling this way because you actually making sure you don't end up with the short stick this time, so cut it out, and inhale this breath taking island."

It was no surprise that Kat was still embracing every moment we was having here. We stayed on our exhaling semi vacation, full of life, bright sun rays that were so embracing I can almost taste the orange beams from it, until the very end, and when it was time to go home, I couldn't wait. I don't know why this was feeling as if I were cheating on Chrome even though I wasn't, but I was glad for it to be over and get back into the security strong arms of my man that loved me and I him. Pressing up against the cool felt glimpse of a window on the plane, whimpering to be home already, I can feel the attitude Kat was giving my lonesome heart. What was I to do, I couldn't help feeling this way, and it should've been a time for me and him, not for me to be with Kat sneaking behind his back, hiding money.

I couldn't be any happier when the plane landed in M.I.A., to be home. Until I saw Six Two waiting for me and Kat at the baggage claim, to take us home. I was hoping to see Chrome, what the hell was Six Two doing here? It only took me a minute to figure out that he chose business once again over me. He had a meeting and nothing not even I could be more important to him when a deal was being made.

Yes I am his main chick, but his status was first in line.

"Welcome back Ms. Brooklynn n Kat, Chrome sent me to make sure you Ladies got home ok."

Six Two greeted us while taking our bags and suitcase to load it on the luggage cart.

"Hello Six Two and where is Mr. Chrome? He wasn't worried enough to come pick me up himself?" I began to interrogate him with a discourage look on my face.

"I am sure he is quite upset he could not pick you up himself, but I also know for a fact he must care about your wellbeing because he sent me to make sure you are safe." Six Two said sternly, coming to Chrome's defense as if he needed one, which again had me in an awkward feeling about why he was not here for me.

When we reached my driveway, Kat nor I could wait to get out and go inside the house, leaving Six Two behind to bring in the luggage.

"Girl, as much as the Islands was good to my body and soul, I am glad to be back on our couch."

Kat exhaled out kicking off her shoes to the side of the front door and plopped herself right down on the couch.

"You are absolutely right my dear, it is great to be home." I replied in agreement with her.

"Well I have brought all the bags in, can I get you anything or do anything else for you Brooklynn."
Six Two asked in an annoying way.

"No, we are good thanks for dropping us home, and tell Chrome don't bother coming over tonight."

"Oh, my bad, I should've mentioned that I am to wait here til he comes. He made it very clear that I was not to leave you alone." Six Two persistently said in an uncomfortable way. I felt like I was under police protection of some sort, and will not stand for this.

"C'mon Kat get up, we have to go, now!" I decided to take matters into my own hands. It was time I get back to my old self and stop allowing Chrome to call all the shots. What was he hiding anyway? It had to be another Woman. Shaking my head and hoping I wasn't going to walk in on another guy breaking my heart was turning me into a hard core non feeling for love at the moment Bitch.

"Where are you going Brooklynn?"
Six Two asked with a confused yet angry look in his face, his height seem to be getting taller by the minute making me feel shorter.

"Well if you must know, I am going to see Chrome, I am not going to wait for him, and you are going to take us there Now!" I ordered him with a little base in my voice, ready to explode into a raging harmonic unstable Woman who has been burned too many times.

"Um-I-um can't let you do that-"
Six Two stopped dead in his tracks of trying to stop
me when I looked at him and pulled out my gun from
my purse, that I just put in there to shoot Chrome's
dick off if he was cheating.

"I *said* let's go!" With that last bold statement,
Six Two wasted no time stepping out of my way and
allowing Kat and I out of the front door, immediately
following behind us and got on the driver side of the
car. He had no choice, no say, no rebuttal, for I was
still holding the gun!

"Brook, you sure you want to do this now? I never
seen you like this before, girl what are you getting
yourself into?" Questions flowed out of Kat with
disbelief of what was in to play with me.

"Kat I am not going through what I went through
with Tony. Do you remember my state of mind I was
in look how long it took me to get back on my feet?
No! I am not going back to that defenseless shell
again. If Chrome is cheating on me, it's all over, but
at least I will walk away with my head high this
time."

I stood on solid ground with my morals, and was
ready to ride it out.

"I'm just saying you going to walk away with
your head high, and some nice silver bracelets, click
clack. You ain't thinking this thing through, or being
rational. Just put the gun down before someone gets
hurt."

I couldn't believe this was my ride or die Kat, what happen to our sisterly bond, she was acting more like me and I her at this moment. The whole time Six Two with his slick ass was driving, but going damn near ten miles under the speed limit, buying his boy time, and I couldn't help but to notice he flinched when I mentioned Tony's name as if he knew him, but he couldn't. They run in different crowds, and I don't remember ever running into Six Two, trust me I would remember this lengthy ass nigga.

"Yo step on it I aint playing around Six. You don't want a bullet in your ass that was meant for Chrome on some cheating shit."
I said to him raising my gun back up showing him I meant business.

"Brooklynn look, no one needs to get hurt here, trust me when I say Chrome is not cheating on you. You got this all wrong, he is in a meeting with some guys he doesn't want you to get involve with, that's all." Six Two stood his ground as well, but I was in no mood to hear anymore bullshit.

"Pull over NOW!"
I threatened Six Two with my gun pointing directly at his head now. He quickly pulled over without any argument.

"Brook, oh my gosh what are you doing?"
Kat nervously asked.

"You too Kat, get out!"

She got out without hesitation too she probably thought I was liable to give her ass a bullet also.

"Now give her the keys, Kat get in the driver seat and Six Two you get in the back, and shut the hell up."

Ordering both of them to do my bidding was the only way I knew to keep in control. I tied Six Two's hand with a silk scarf I had in my purse, which mind you he could've over take both Kat and I, but I guess he said it wouldn't be worth it, he almost look like he was enjoying the mental break down I seemed to be having. Then I balled up his handkerchief he had sticking out of his black suit, and stuck it in his mouth. Right now I didn't want to hear any more of his attempts to cover for Chrome. Kat nervously took over the wheel and headed us straight to Chrome's place. When we got there I sat for a minute to gather my thoughts.

"What do you want to do now Brooklynn?" Kat asked me using my full name, which only meant one thing she was still scared and worried about what I would do next.
"You stay here and keep an eye on Six Two, I will handle this by myself."

I looked in Six Two's glove compartment and just knew he had a glock. I handed it to Kat for her to stay behind and watch Six Two. Then I approached the house and unlock the door with my key sneaking in and staying quiet. I walked in staying close to the walls, getting closer to voices coming from Chrome's dining room. Before I just bust out on his rendezvous like a crazy bitch with a gun, something stopped me dead in my tracks. It was a voice that I recognize, a corny cocky sounding guy. It was HEAT! As soon as I figured out who Chrome meeting was with, there was no reason for him to know that I was there. Heat knew me, he knows that I dated Tony, and I really don't want that part of my life interfering with my new life. Little did I know then that was inevitable.

"All I need from you Chrome is for your men to handle this loose end for me, and I will have no problem giving you fifteen percent of my take."

Heat was talking about a deal with Chrome, but I also wondered why Chrome didn't mention this meeting with me. I thought he wanted me on all the business. I continued to stay behind the door, and listen in on their conversation.

"I don't know Heat, fifteen percent sounds like crap for what I am about to do for you, I could easily loose the most important thing in my life doing this job." Chrome debating back to Heat about the deal, and what was he talking about that he could lose. I guess I really didn't know Chrome like I thought I did.

"Chrome my man, you run a hard bargain, ok how about this, I'll give you twenty five percent of my next take, and you can run all of Carol City too, but I need assurance that his will be done as soon as possible, I just can't let people think less of me if I let this nigga get away with this shit."

"I understand, and I agree with the deal before me, so you have my word, and it will be done. Now if you don't mind, let's wrap this up, my Lady is coming back today and she can be a hard ass if I neglect her."

Chrome took Heat's deal and joked with him as he shook his hand while having one of the guys walked him out. In fear of Kat getting caught with Six Two indispose, I texted her right before the two men came out of the room for her to drive around the block, so Heat wouldn't see them. I waited until it was clear and then popped in the living room as if I had just walked in the house and had no idea what was going on.

"Brook? What are you doing here baby? I told Six Two to make sure you get home safe, and that I would be come over when you were unpacked and relaxed."

Chrome was surprised to see me, and did not even mention his meeting with Heat, but that's ok because I will find out on my own what this meeting was about.

"Well, Six Two tried his hardest to make me stay home, waiting on you, but I wasn't feeling that shit. So I made Kat drive me up here and both of them are in the car."

I took off my blue suit jacket with a gold trim and threw it on the couch as a sign of my irritable mood, as I answered him. Keeping in mind that Heat just walked out of here and hoped that he doesn't run into

Kat in the dark tinted black cougar car driving Six Two around.

"Well I for one am glad to see you, and so glad your home." He said smiling, coming towards me for a warm welcome embrace, but I quickly turned away, thinking about what kind of business he had with Heat.

"Are you really glad to see me? I mean you weren't there to pick me up at the Airport. What was so important that you had to send Six Two to pick me up?" I bombarded him with jealous questions to throw him off of me knowing about his meeting with Heat.

"Awe, is my Brook Baby feeling a little insecure? That's not like you honey, you know you are the only woman that can handle a man like me."

He was feeling himself too much for my liking, but I would let him have his moment as I allow him to console what he thought was my insecurities, however this was not the end. Deceitfulness started to turn in my head, and as I sensually pressed up against his strong frame hugging him close to me I could feel his manhood rise. It only assured me he was being truthful about missing me, but it was not enough for me to keep my eyes from narrowing behind his head and allowing scrutiny to invade my thoughts.

"Hmmm, I did miss you Brook Baby, your smell on my pillow was beginning to fade. Let's go upstairs and spread your enticing scent back all over my bed."

Chrome was in the mood for a great fuck, but I was in no mood to entertain him until I know what the hell is going on.

"As tempting as that sounds *Babe*, we still have a problem. Uh, I got Kat outside with a gun to Six Two's head, and yeah, sorry guess my insecurities are more troublesome than I care to admit."

I ratted out myself breaking all of Chrome's sexual concentration on my ass. He pulled away from me in disbelief, looking me up and down and then walking over to the front window, but couldn't see anything except me standing there with my arms folded in a taunt stance as if I did nothing that wasn't expected. He headed for the front door and pulled it opened almost seeming mad as hell, I followed behind just to make sure he don't take his anger out on Kat.

"What the hell were you thinking, Brooklynn? Six Two could of easily put a bullet in you!"

I don't know whether to be mad at Chrome for talking to me in an angry Father tone, or to feel relieved that he seemed to be more concern about my wellbeing than Six Two's.

"Well gee Chrome, I was thinking you sent your guard dog to keep me at bay, and I ain't falling for the bullshit while you might've been in pussy land with some fucked up thirsty bitch!"

Not giving him any room to be right in this, I stood my ground and planted my heels. He gave me an uncertain look and I shrugged my shoulders, then he pulled open the driver side of the door causing Kat to almost fall out.

"Oh shit! I told you Brook this was a bad idea, you never listen to your girl."
Kat wasted no time selling me out.

"Really Kat? You can cut the act out, I told Chrome this was all me, so just chill for a moment."

Kat hung her head in shame when she heard I already had her back. When Chrome opened the back door and saw Six Two, he took out the scarf from Six Two's mouth and to my surprise both of them began laughing.

"What the fuck is so funny?"

My anger was no match to the humor they found themselves in.

"Six, my man, you did good. Thanks for allowing my girl to bitch you up."
Chrome knew exactly that his boy was in no danger with me, and I him. It was clear that Six Two went along just to please me, but if I had been anybody else, this whole thing could've turned ugly.

"Awwe, Brook Baby don't be mad, you are so damn sexy when your lip pokes out like that."

Chrome smiling back at me putting his finger in front of my lips that I felt like biting that shit off!

"Glad you and your boy is having a great reunion, Kat and I are heading back home. I can't be around you two right now."

My mood was not the happiest, and I did not want to stay and give Chrome my goodies right now, he needed to know how hurt I was about the whole secrecy and James Bond shit he had Six Two put on. Getting in the car without another word to Chrome, I signaled for Kat to get in, and we reversed out of the wide long driveway leaving them niggas to laugh as we drove off in Six Two's car.

CHAPTER 6: PLANTING THE SEED

"It has been three days Brook, when are you going to stop pacing the floor and call Chrome and give up the pussy so both of us can be happy again?"

Kat asked annoyed by my behavior since we came from our trip. The problem was she had no idea what I was fuming about, to her Chrome wasn't cheating and I was overreacted, but the fact remains that Heat was at his house which didn't leave a good taste in my mouth at all.

"Kat I need your full attention on this one. Try to follow me while I tell you what really happened that day with Chrome."

I began explaining to her about the details of that day. Kat Instantly stopped filing her long claw like nails to sit up on our couch and give me her undivided attention.

"When I walked in his house that day, he didn't see me right away. He was still in his meeting with someone we both know very well."

Laying it on her thick was the only way I knew how to lead up to tell her who Chrome was meeting that day.

"Chrome had a meeting with Heat!"
I exclaimed to her, however her reaction was not what I would expect. She looked more confused than ever.
"Oh k, he was meeting with Heat, and?"

Kat asked clueless to the connection, I would have to spell it out for her.

"Heat the boyfriend of the girl who I caught Tony with. Big time grimy ass mutha fucka coke dealer, *that Heat*."

"I know which Heat you're talking about Brook, I'm saying, so what? What is the big idea if Heat and Chrome link up? Doesn't that just mean more money coming to everybody?"
It was plain to see that Kat only thought of them being together was good for business.

"If this was any other guy maybe it wouldn't fucking phase me, but the fact that it is Heat, and the fact that Chrome didn't want to tell me, or even the fact that he wants Chrome to do some dirty ass work for him, just don't sit right with me."
My head was spinning from stressing out over this shit, but I needed to know what the big deal was, and then I saw Kat sitting there still not catching on, and just like that it came to me, I would set Kat up with Heat to find out what's going on. Heat would have no reason not to trust Kat, she would approach him like she did most of her dudes in the club, bent over, sexed up with her own stacks, appealing to his eye for some caramel chocolate pussy he can add to his trophy

shelf of exotic women. With one brow raised and a smirk on my face staring at Kat as live bait scared the shit out of her.

"Oh no you don't, I know that look. You are not involving me in any of your sneaky schemes. I still have emotional scars from the last scheme you pulled when I had to cover for you and Tony sneaking away for a weekend to go to a concert all the way in New York when we were kids. You remember what happened then don't you? Your Moms found out and sent your Dad over to my house to grill me, he had me in tears for a week. Brook I break under pressure."

Kat was pleading for mercy, but the more she talked the more I wanted her to get in good with Heat so I could find out everything I need.

"Girl what happen to my ride or die chica? We in this together, I will not let anything happen to you, all I need is for you to drop that sunshine gold pussy on Heat long enough to find out where he plays at, what he's plotting with Chrome. C'mon I need you, I can't trust anyone else."
Looking straight into Kat's blue eyes that were obviously contacts along with her long eye lashes, I begged her with my sad puppy dog look, probably the same one I gave her back then when I asked her to cover for me.

"Brook you better have my back this time, cuz I swear if I have to take another lecture for you, and not even by your Dad but by your Man, girl I will be bringing you down with me. Fine I'll do it, but I am going to need a new wardrobe, some money to flash around, and a new ride." She wasted no time using this as a perfect moment to reinvent herself at the mall. I shook my head at her, letting her know that I will handle all the details down to the moment where she would just happen to be in Heat's view. The one major thing I had for insurance was the fact that neither Chrome nor Heat would be aware of my suspicion.

Getting Kat all the material things she would need to pull this off such as, dressy fur vests, slinky dazzled low cut dresses, six to eight inch stilettos, I know Heat likes his women tall, he was not a looker, nor did he have swag, but in his world money talk and bullshit, well you get it. Heat mostly wore suits with no shirt underneath, he preferred sneakers instead of the usual gator skin shoes guys in his profession wears. His shoulder length blond hair was dyed for the surf boarder look he was going for. I don't know much about his background except for the fact Tony knew that he pretty much inherited money, and Heat love women to floss around him more than jewelry. I do know that he can smell a gold digger a mild away, which confused me why he would have that bitch Sugar Cane around. There was one last thing I needed to give Kat to complete her style.

"Oh my gosh Brook, is this mine? I have to give her a name, this red beauty Porsche convertible looks like a Michelle."

Kat fell in love with her new ride as soon as I had the dealer drive it up to the house.

"Now remember Kat, don't come on to him, let him come to you. Make it hard for him to catch you, then when he is falling all over you, keep one ear open for his meetings, If Chrome shows up, stay out of site, and text me any information you get don't matter if you think it will help or not, and don't forget to delete them. You hear me?"

I grabbed her arm making her comprehend what I was telling her. She was too wrapped up by the sight of the car.

"Yes I hear you girl, I know what I am doing, and you should know better, I don't fall for men, only women."

"Don't get caught up with the women there either." I warned Kat, knowing that pussy is the only thing that can distract her. Before sending her off to do my bidding, I stood for a moment and wonder if this was worth getting into, but no time to back down. It's time for me to grow a thick skin and be the Woman that Chrome taught me to be. Waving to my girl as I watch her drive off sending her into the arms of what soon would be my number one enemy.

It has been a week already since Kat has been gone, and still no word from her. I hope everything was ok with her. The house seemed empty and lonely without her or Chrome for that matter. I haven't called him since the incident, I wanted him to understand how heated I was about the situation he put me in. Yet I can't help but miss his seducing eyes, and his kissable lips, the way his hands felt so strong when he would grab me and pull me close to him, falling all over his intensity. Just as I seemed to start masturbating lying on my bed thinking of Chrome, my cell phone starts vibrating. Hurrying to go pick it up thinking it was Kat, I felt a blush of heat fill my cheeks as I saw it was Chrome calling.

"Hello."

I anxiously said.

"B, what you doing tonight?" Chrome asked in a cunning way, as if he knew I have been over here missing him.

"I have no plans. My man laid me out to dry. Why do you want to take over where he left off?" I responded back to him playing along with his insidious way.

"It sounds like you need to get that sexy low cut in the back black dress on that I like, and those red bottom heels, then get your sexy ass in the car and come on over here now."

He required me to his cravings, and it became obvious that he was missing me just as much. Without any more talk or hesitation, I quickly hung up the phone, got dressed, pulled my hair up into a sleek up do hair style, showing off my neck line for an inviting intent of seduction foreplay. I finished off with my body spray from Victoria's Secret. My sensual silhouette was begging for intimacy with Chrome tonight, and I for one did not want to disappoint him.

Pulling up to his house so late at night intimidated me a little. It looked so gloomy and dark like a scary castle in the middle of Liberty City, and still I proceeded to go in. I mean after all I had my own key.

"You look good enough to eat. Maybe would should just skip dinner and go right to breakfast." Chrome complimented my appetizing appearance.

"Lucky for you I had dinner already, but I am always ready to feed you." I said toying back with him, as I pressed in close to him for a greeting kiss and playfully biting his bottom lip, all to lead us up to his room. Chrome, wearing nothing but a white wife beater T-shirt on showing his six packs through, and gray baggy jogging pants that made me think he just came from the gym looking all pumped up. He picked me up and carried me to the bedroom, he slowly opened the door, and there were rose petals of all colors, red, pink, white, and purple, sprinkled on the floor and on our bed. He had candles burning in every inch of the room. I was impressed that he took time to make our little reunion special.

"My woman deserves to walk on rose petals."

He whispered in my ear giving me goose bumps as he put me down to stand up. The feel of walking on rose petals was enjoyable to my feet, and I felt like a Queen.

"Wow Chrome, you have really out done yourself this time." I complimented him with love in my eyes.

"This is just the beginning of what I have planned for you." He said in a low voice. Then he walked over to his dark oak wood polish finish armoire, opened the top draw and took out what looks like a *silver rose*? I walked over to him curious to see what it was. He took my hand and said,

"Brook, you have been good to me, and for me. I see you and me building a big life together, with everything and everyone at our feet. I want you by my side, through thick and thin, us having kids."
I was in shock by his words, and was he trying to ask me to-
"I guess what all of this is leading too is, Brook will you make an honest man out of me?"

Chrome just popped out the main question any woman would be jumping for joy to hear, and I was. He handed me the silver rose with a long stem, it was actually a ring box, and when I opened it there was a breath taking Blue Diamond ring setting on platinum with five karat white Diamonds on the band. He slipped it on my finger, and with the whole moment I totally forgot about Kat and my distrust in Chrome, when all he wanted to do was keep me happy. He took the ring out the box and slid it on my finger, and I stood there saying nothing, just in awe of the moment. It felt good on my finger, giving me chills up and down my spine, and it brought an unintentional big smile to my face.

"I-I don't know what to say, this is unexpected." I proclaim to him, yet still smiling at the ring.

"You can say yes, and make me the happiest man in Miami." He said to me holding my hands and looking into my eyes with his hypnotic way. Once again I found myself unable to say no to him.

"Nothing would make me happier than to be your wife."
And with that answer *I signed my life away on the dotted line* to him. I laid the biggest juiciest softest kiss on him. His hands felt soft against the middle of my back as he gently glides his fingers up and down. Our bodies were in sync with the moment, and our passion for each other took over. I started ripping his t-shirt off of him initiating him to take his turn. He grabbed my legs and lifted me up. Straddling him with my legs I continued to kiss, suck, and taste his neck. He walked over to the dresser, using one hand to hold me, and the other to swipe all the stuff off of the dresser. Chrome then sat me up on it, pulling down my red laced panties, and I became aroused by his forcefulness. Every movement seemed timeless yet we were moving so fast, in a rush to get inside each other. I had my arms around his waist, his

hands were grabbing my ass, I pushed down his jogging pants, and he positioned me on him. He was kissing, sucking and licking my nipples, while I was grinding, riding, and sliding up and down on him. We were so into it that I was literally all on him, not on the dresser anymore. We didn't stop there, he wanted more of me, I wanted more of him. I came down off of him. He playfully pushed me against the wall facing it. I could feel once again his strong hard dick as he pressed it up against me from behind, trying to come in through the back door, and with an inhale of excitement we were having orgasmic, screaming, moaning, hard core fucking, and passionate sex.

Several hours later, after the emotions ran out of us completely, we were laying there breathless in each other's arms. I gazed once again at my ring, and for the first time since I left Tony I felt a real peace. A perfect moment in time, but before I can let myself go off into a bliss of matrimony I suddenly remembered Kat! First thing tomorrow, I will call Kat and tell her she's off the hook concerning Heat, and just as I was about to doze off in Chromes arms, his phone started to vibrate. He got up to look at it, making me feel uncomfortable about the fact that this was our night, a special night, I mean he did ask me to marry him, which in any man's book is a big deal too, and now he is checking his messages. Fury started to overtake my loving feeling towards him once again.

"Who was that?" I asked in an annoying girlfriend way.

"Sorry Babe, it's Six Two. I got to take care of some business. Urghh, oh shit, I don't want to leave your sexy ass, but some real messed up shit is going down." He grunted about leaving, and still he was getting up to go in the shower and leave me, here, alone, with a ring on my finger. Maybe this is what he thinks marrying me will be like. That it will be ok for him to just get up and handle business in the middle of the night. I am not with that, all feelings has just walked out the door behind him.

"I won't be hear when you get back Chrome!" I shouted from his room out to him as I got up to go take a shower.

"What the hell is that supposed to mean Brook?" He asked coming back into the room seeming to be mad as hell at me.

"It means that I am going home. If you can get up and leave just like that after the night we just had, I am going home. It obviously didn't mean anything to you. I am not staying here alone while you parade the streets with your goons. I am not looking forward to living life this way with you. So do me a favor, and when you are finish playing King of the streets, give me a call until then, Chrome, I can't marry you."

I almost choked on the last part, however he needed to know where I am coming from, and even though I threatened not to marry him, there was no need for me to give back the ring, or throw it at him, no, me keeping this ring will hurt him more, and keep me warm at nights while he makes his decision.

"Hold on Brook, don't leave like this baby, I am really sorry. This was a special night for both of us, but I need you by my side, here in my house, on the other side of my bed, with me. Look take a nice hot bath in the Jacuzzi, get a bottle of my reserved champagne from the gallery down stairs, release some of that tension I felt when we made love, and before you know it I will be back home, and I'll make a promise to you, I will let these niggas know that after 9 p.m. all calls are done. No more business while I am home with you. I want this to work Baby, I need you in my life."

He sweet talked his way to my heart, kissing me on my forehead. I could yell at him, be a hard ass, but instead, I'll take him up on his offer, lay back and watch him, and the first wrong move he makes I'm out of here.

I stood there in the room wrapped in his sheets clinching to it at the top of my breast, still furiated, but never the less I would stay behind. As I started to run my bath I decided to call Kat and see how she was handling things, and since Chrome had my senses on alert, I would let her finish what we started. I called her phone, but it just went straight to her voice mail. I remember distinctively telling Kat to keep in touch with me so I know she was ok. Right before I was about to turn off my phone and set it down, my phone notified me of 4 unread messages, they were from Kat! I must have missed them during my love session with Chrome. So she was ok, maybe she was messaging me about all the sexy girls, or how all the men were falling over her, shaking my head to myself I put the phone down, and decided to go enjoy a glass of champagne in the hot tub first, and then entertain myself later with her adventure messages while I wait for Chrome's return.

The hot bath was just what I needed. I got out, with steam rising from my body. I grabbed my monogram towel with my initials on it that Chrome had ordered for me when we first started dating, and I put it on. Walking over to the bedroom, I sat on the bed drying my hair, and turned on the TV. Even though everything at the moment seems to be right, my cell phone kept staring at me begging for me to read Kat's messages. She probably was having the time of her life at one of Heat's big party, and decided to send me pictures. I had nothing better at the moment to do so I decided to open the messages.

Kat   Yesterday 9:15 PM

Brook,
Girl, you were right. There are some crazy ties between Chrome Peeps and Heat. Well I don't know why you can't pick up your phone, so I'll just let you in on what's going on. Heat right now is with Six Two, I had to stay hidden so he doesn't see me. I heard Heat tell Six Two that Tony would be at his party tomorrow night. That he had hired him, but Tony doesn't know that Heat found out about Tony sleeping with his woman.
I got a bad feeling about this, hmu, or get your ass here tomorrow.

Kat's message threw me all off of range. I had to read the rest of her messages. It sounds like they setting up for revenge on Tony for Heat.... That party is tonight! Chrome just left, he lied to me. I opened up the second message.

Kat   yesterday 11:59 PM

Damn Brooklynn, why haven't you hit me back yet. As I was sneaking out of the room trying not to be seen, I dropped my cell phone because I was shaken, but I didn't turn back in fear of Six Two recognizing me, which he probably did already. Any way it was too risky to go back downstairs to see what was going on. So I'm up here in one of Heat's ho's room, I know you told me to leave them girls alone but hell I was horny, anyway she said I could hang out there, but you need to get here, you need to come get me out of this shit NOW!

Kat's sounded scared as hell in her second message, oh fuck what was I to do, this all went down last night, well maybe she was worried about nothing because there were two remaining text from her. I decided to get dress and go see what the hell was going on, but not before I checked out the two remaining messages from her.

Kat   Today 6 PM

Brook, I am so fucking scared right now, where are you, call me. Heat found me and told me to stay in his room, he got some nigga watching the door, I can't escape. He hit me a couple of times and ask me what I was doing there, and where my phone was, I had told him I left it in the girls room, when he dragged me out, but I had it hidden in my breast

when I heard him coming. What should I do? Get
your ass here now!!

Kat   Today 8:32
PM

This maybe my last message to you Brook, I am now
in the trunk of Heats car they blind folded me,
thinking I won't know it's Six Two and Chrome's
Goons, but I know his smell anywhere, that damn
cheap ass cool waters wearing nigga, lifted me up and
I felt I was high up in the air. I don't know where
they're taking me or what's gonna happen to me but
I know it something bad. I will leave my phone on in
hopes you can follow my gps. I downloaded it in your
phone when we had this planned just in case, so
follow it......   I love you girl.

I felt a sharp pain in the pit of my stomach, I had put
my girl in danger, and tears filled up my eyes like a
raging river. I was mad, hurt, sad, betrayed, taken
for granted, and everyone that I trusted was now my
enemy, and Chrome being number one on my list. I
hit my gps app, and hit find Kat's phone, it started
beeping in the location of Alligators Alley Highway!

I grabbed my gun loaded it, picked up my Keys and
purse, and headed for my ride. I had to think for a
moment though. Tony was in trouble too. I couldn't
be in two places at once. So I called him right away,
and just like I knew he would pick up on the first
ring, he did.

"Hey, Brook?" He sounded happy and confused at the same time to find out I was calling him.

"Listen to me Tony, I don't have time right now but I need you to meet me at Alligator Alley right now!"

The only way I knew to get Tony out of this jam and still get my girl Kat was to have him meet me.

"Brook, I so want to see you, but I got this gig, I'm on my way there now, hey why don't you come over there and meet me, it's at Heat's house."

Tony was not as smart as I give him credit to be. I had to spell everything out for him.

"Tony, I don't know how to tell you this, but you have to believe me it's a setup, don't go! Heat knows about you and Sugar Cane. He wants you dead. Just meet me now and I'll explain the rest when I get there."

By the dead silence on the phone I got from Tony's end I knew he got how urgent and serious I was.

"Al-alright, I'm on my way."
As soon as I hung up from him Chrome called me, I debated on whether I should answer him or not. In my calm mind with the wheels turning I answered the phone and pretend to not know anything so that I can find out what he knows.

"Hello?"

"Hey B, I was calling to say sorry again for having to leave you, but just wanted to check up on you. I will be home in a while."
He was being slick too, he probably wanted to know if I knew about Kat being found out.

"Oh hey, I am not mad anymore, and I thought maybe I would start moving in tonight. I'm heading home right now to pack a suit case, unless you don't want me to move in."
I thought if I played the dumb blond routine he might get less suspicious of me, and maybe even Kat, and let her go.

"Woww, of course not, you want me to come help?"
He asked in curiosity maybe, but I wouldn't let my guard down either.

"No it's ok hun, you finish your business, cause when I get back, it's just me and you."

I was even amazed at my deception, but hey I learned from the best, him.

"Sounds good B, ok I'll hurry back home then and prepare a lil something for you."

He was so wrapped up by my cunning way he couldn't see the monster he created in me.

CHAPTER 8 THE ULTIMATE BETRAYAL

I drove all the way to Alligators Alley weaving in and out of traffic. As I got closer the gps sensor beeped louder, and my heart was sinking faster. I hope to get to her before anything bad happens, and yet I was scared to death, would it just be me and her against Chrome, Six Two and their Goons. Really I couldn't take anymore conclusion jumping. It was dark on Alligator Alley, and the worst part is that you never want to get a flat tire on this road, for the simple fact that it was named for Alligator territory. Oh no, Kat, Alligators, I stepped on the gas harder to get to her faster. Finally the gps stopped at a cut off in the road, it was dark but no cars or no one was in site. Before getting out my ride, I tried to text her phone to see if she was still in the trunk of the car. I waited about three minutes but no answer. Ok, I thought to myself, it's now or never. As I got out of my Jeep, I took my gun and put it in the back of my jeans. Turning on my phone again, I decided to call instead of text maybe I could hear her phone ringing, but it was so dark I had no flashlight, there could be an Alligator waiting to eat me, and then I almost jumped out of my skin when I felt someone touch the back of my shoulder.

"Hey it's ok, it's just me Tony. You want to tell me why we are out here in the middle of Alligator territory?" Thank God it was Tony, and he looked more scared than I felt.

"I'm glad it's you. Look I need you to help me find Kat, she is out here somewhere, and it's a long story, but please you got to help me find her."

Sounding desperate I pleaded for Tony's help.

"Kat? What is she doing out here at this time of night? Look Brooklynn I have no problem helping you find her, but it's dark, and we could get eaten alive out here, and you still aint tell me what you know about Heat and him wanting to kill me."

Tony was making it hard for me to appreciate him coming out here, but he did have a point, this just wasn't the time for chit chat.

"If you want to stand out here and wait, then go ahead, but I am going to look for Kat!"
Standing my ground, I sternly said to Tony. It was just like the old days when we disagree and I would storm off.

"What kind of man would I be to let you go off by yourself? You don't know what's out there."
He said to me turning on his flashlight app on his phone and leading the way holding my hand behind him.

I followed him, still calling Kat's phone. I didn't even warn Tony that we might run into trouble with Chrome's men. We walked about five hundred yards into some wooded area away from the cut off on the highway, when I heard the faint ring of Kat's phone.

"We must be getting closer." I said to Tony, clutching on to him tighter, getting worried about what we might have to deal with. The phone got louder and louder til we saw an abandon blue sedan. We looked in it, in the trunk, and still no sign of Kat.

"I don't understand where she can be." I said to Tony, confused and worried about not finding Kat, yet her phone was in the trunk of the car, so I knew we were in the right place.

"She is over here Brook!" Tony shouted to me sounding relieved that we found her.

"Wait, you shouldn't see her like this. Go get the truck." Tony stopped me from getting close to Kat, initializing that I shouldn't see Kat because something was terribly wrong.

"What the hell do you mean? Move out of my way Tony." I ignored his warning pushing him off of me to get to Kat. I gasped at first glance, she was covered in blood, and her lifeless naked body was lying on the ground. She was still breathing, I could see her chest barely rising I rush to her side wanting to take away her pain, shaking my head in disbelief that this came from the hands of Chrome. Tony called the police and ambulance right away. After thirty seven minutes of waiting and praying over Kat's body for God not to take her away from me, the ambulance and police finally arrived. Everything seemed blurry and in slow motion with the harsh cold rain falling on and all around us, washing the blood from Kat's body onto the ground and rolling down to the river below us. My arms were still clinched tightly around her broken body, when the Paramedics got to us. They worked around me to stabilize her as much as they could before taking her slowly away from me and putting her on the stretcher. A cop that was talking with Tony came over to me with a spear jacket and put it around me. My hair was drenched and my heart had been beaten up as badly as Kat body looked, all I could do was stand in the rain trying to figure all this bull shit out, and then my emotions turned from sadness, and lowliness, to raging fury and vengeful determination that all will pay for what they have done. I had nothing to say to the cops, and Tony explained to them that it may not be the right time. I got in my jeep to follow behind the ambulance Tony said he would meet up with me there, after answering as much questions he could to the police, but I knew he would not reveal who exactly was responsible, it all goes with the Durty South territory to keep it in the streets, no snitches or consider your family and friends no more. I left behind a total chaos of confused officials, and a tow truck rigging up a car not too far from where we found Kat laying, guess the dumb asses that Chrome hired to do the job didn't think the cops would find it, or Kat for that matter. Driving crazy like a mad woman behind the ambulance in the heavy rain, all kinds of shit was running through my mind, Kat, Tony, Heat, and most of all Chrome! What was I going to do about this situation and there is no way I could let them slide away. After all it's my girl who paid for all my suspicion and she did it for me. First thing is first, I am going to get Heat for this shit, it was his call, he was the one who ask for Kat's blood, I am almost sure of it, and then I'll take care of them so called dogs on leashes. Six Two may be a problem, but he is on my hit list. Chrome, I am saving him for last, I still can't believe he went behind my back and hurt my girl, he didn't even tell me that Heat was on her, and he didn't ask me what was going on before he just laid down like a bitch and took it in the ass from Heat to go behind my back and hurt my heart. He wasn't the man I thought he was. He wasn't the guy I met at the gas station taking me on exotic trips and dates promising never to hurt me or break my heart. He was now my number one Enemy, and his last gift from me will be the sweetest vengeful shit any woman scorned could come up with.

When we finally reached the hospital, the paramedics took Kat in on the stretcher quickly. I followed behind them as nurses and a Doctor ran up to her gurney and started procedure care on her.

"Ma'am I will need you to step out of the room. Are you family?"

One of the nurses asked me, attempting to move me out of the room. I stood there in frozen time watching all the commotion going on over my best friends lifeless body, my number one girl, my ride or die bitch, friends til the end, and then I responded,

"Yes I am family, she is my sister."
I said with tears rolling down once again, I can feel rage building up and burning my eyes from the whole ordeal I got Kat in.

"I am sorry, but we will try to do everything to save her, we just need you to step out of the room."

The nurse proceeded to get me out of the room, but like a stubborn bull I refuse to budge. I left Kat once, and look what happened, I was not about to leave her again.

"I am not leaving this room, She is all I have, so go and help her, I don't care what the cost, if you need to fly a mutha fucking specialist down here to save her get your ass on that phone and do it now, but don't tell me to leave one more time, or you going to be laid out right next to my girl!" All obscenities, and rage poured out of me, and made the nurse shrink two sizes, but she left me alone and went back to helping the other nurses and the Doctor to save my Kat.

They continued to stop her bleeding, attaching IV's to her hand because her arm was so bruised up they couldn't get a viable vein, and I stood there just praying, praying that she will be alright, praying that she can forgive me, praying that I find these fucked up bastards and kill them before someone else gets the chance. A few minutes later Tony finally made it to the hospital and was standing by my side holding my hand showing his support. I needed his support, I needed him by my side, I needed him at that right moment, but not sexually, just him.

"Well is she going to be alright?" He asked me still holding my hands.

"I don't know, they just working as fast as they can, doing the best they can, but I just don't know Tony. This is entirely my fault I had no right to send her blindly into the arms of a psychopath."

My voice started to tremble and I began to cry on Tony's shoulder, he in return consoled me, rubbing my shoulders in his understanding way.

"Don't go blaming yourself Brook, you had no idea this was going to happen, and I am sure she will be ok, Kat is a hard rock, you're a hard rock, she usually takes care of you, but now you have to be here for her." Tony had the right words coming out of his mouth, and I always did love that about him. This moment however, would not change the fact of why we broke up in the first place, so I still didn't feel the need to get back romantically with him.

"Brooklynn right? Your Sister is going to need surgery, there is some internal bleeding and fractured bones, her nose needs to be reset, but I promise that I will do my best to save her. I know you don't want to leave her side, my nurse already warned me of that, but in order for me to save your sister, I will need to have only the nurses and the anesthesiologist in the room with me, there is a room above the surgery where you can sit and watch everything."

The Doctor filled me in on Kat's condition, and I guess if I want her back I had to compromise, I nodded at him that I will go to the room, and then I grabbed his arm,

"You bring her back to me, alive, do what you have to do and save her!" I said to him with a deep look in my eyes jabbing him in the chest with my pointer finger. Then Tony and I headed for the room with the glass view of the surgery.

We watched for several hours, praying, holding hands, and Tony never hesitated during the procedure to console me at times when it was touch and go with Kat, as the doctors worked hard on her. They sewed and stitched up her wounds. Her nose had to be reset, and they mended her broken ribs. Why did they have to hurt my girl like she was some fucking dude? Were they so intimidated by a woman that they felt the need to fuck her up like their real enemies? Shaking my head and resting it on Tony was all I could do now.

"Brook, I think there done baby." Tony said nudging my head lightly with his shoulder, looking down at the nurses who seemed to be cleaning up and putting away the bloody surgical tools that were used on Kat's body. I looked at the Doctor with puppy dog eyes praying for the best, he looked up at me, and nodded his head as a notion that everything went good. A slight smile came to my face but she still was not out of danger.

CHAPTER 9 A NEW LESSON IN THE GAME

After a brief talk with the Doctor, I was assured that Kat would need a lot of rest, and it will take her a long time to heal, not just physically but mentally too. Tony left the hospital when she came out of surgery to get us some food and a change of clothes for me so that I could stay by her side and be there when she woke up. The last thing Kat would need is too wake up traumatized and no one by her side to comfort her.

It had been two days already and no sign of Kat waking up, I was getting worried that she might slip into a coma and never wake up, which was the only concern the Doctor had for Kat. He said sometimes an ordeal like this patients couldn't handle and slipped away in their self-consciousness. I wouldn't allow it though, if she wouldn't wake up I might have to slap her out of it, I needed her to come back to me.

Laying by her bed that night I fell asleep holding her hand, and she had to feel my vibe, because around two thirty in the morning I felt a slight squeeze around my hand that woke me up. Feeling kind of out of it, I thought maybe I was dreaming, but when I looked at Kat, I saw her eyes rolling under eyelids and slowly opening. Once she opened her big beautiful light brown eyes, I smiled at her with a tear rolling down my face, she tried to smile back but I could see the pain in her face when she couldn't. She didn't speak right away, but she moved her hand slowly out from under mine to point to the pitcher of ice cold water that sat on the table next to her bed that the nurses had filled up overnight. Realizing it was water that she was signaling for I poured her a cup and put a straw in it so she wouldn't have to lift her bandaged head up too much. She took a long sip and then signal for me to put it back on the table, and before I could say anything she looked at me and gave me a stronger smile,

"Girl you look like shit, you look as bad as when I found you crying over Tony in the hotel room."

It was only so Kat like for her first words to be critical of my running mascara, dirty face look from crying over here, instead of a normal person who might have just said hey, I'm glad to see you. I chuckled a bit to her as I tried to wipe my face with a handkerchief.

"Glad to see they didn't mess with your personality in surgery honey." Making small talk with her to break the isolation, feeling sick to my stomach for being the reason she was here in the first place.

"Well you know what they say you can't keep a bad chick down." She winked her eye at me cunningly.

"Hey Kat girl, I am glad to see that you are finally awake." Smiling on the outside greeting her with my heart, but still dying on the inside from the pain I put her in.

"How are you feeling? Do you want me to get the Doctors?"

"I feel like shit, which is how I probably look, but no I don't want those white jacket wearing fools in here. I am just glad you found me Brook, but every time I close my eyes, they are going to be there, my nightmares will make me relive it over and over again. What am I gonna do, what if they find out that I am still alive and come back to finish the job."

Kat sounded like her soul was not rested and she was being tormented by the sick goons who did this shit to her. Only I could write this wrong....

"Look, all I want you to do is rest, let me worry about all that, you need to save your strength and get back better, and Tony and I will take turns watching over you, besides, no one knows we found you, not Heat and I sure as hell ain't telling Chrome. I need you to get better though, and I promise you we are getting the fuck out of dodge, with so much money you will never have to work at a strip club again baby doll." I set forth a good statement, and besides the wheels began to turn in my vengeful mind, and a master plan was being conceived. I became a soldier at war now.

Kat fell back asleep, the meds kept her in solitude allowing her body to heal, and over the next few days I stayed by her side, and when I had to maintain my wifey duty's to Chrome so he don't get suspicious of my whereabouts Tony stood in my place by Kat's hospital bed side, but it was getting harder to keep going back and forth.

"Tony it's good to see you and Brooklynn together again, even though you are not really together. I just feel like y'all are family."

Kat smiled up and noted her observance of us over the few days at Tony who was standing by her hospital bed side, feeding her lunch.

"We will always be family, all three of us, Brook and I may never get back where we were, or together for that matter, but we have a bond between us that will never break. You know sometimes you can be a pain in my ass back in the day, but I wouldn't rather be anywhere else but right here by your side."

He replied with a high spirit and even a little bit of jokes with his appreciation towards my best friend. They were ol friends again, when I walked in her room with a vase full of violet daisies her favorite.

"What are you two crazies talking bout? Here girl these are for you, hope they brighten up your room a bit." It was nice to see my x and my girl getting along especially under the circumstances. It was time though to make moves.

"Thank you Brook, and to be honest these four walls are a drag to look at every day, I feel like I am getting better, so when the hell are you getting me out of here." Nothing can keep Kat at bay too long and she didn't like to feel caged up. I knew it would only be so long before she would get the itch to leave.

"Way ahead of you girl, Tony and I got a nice condo on Brickell Ave. facing the water for you. We also hired you a physical therapy nurse to help you get back on your feet."

I began to bring the news I hoped that would cheer her up, and start to repair the damage I cause.

"Yeah Kat, and I know a bouncer that owes me a favor, and he will watch and protect over you when either one of us can't be with you, so you will never be alone." Tony assured her with his way of protection. I still was amazed that he stayed, and he believed me without a doubt when I called him about Heat setting him up. He really was a stand up man in the end.

"I have only one question for the both of y'all is my nurse cute?" We all looked at each other and laughed, and at that moment I knew we were ok.

It took all but a week to get everything settled in Kat's new place for her, and yes we got her a sexy nurse, but our main concern was to get her back on her feet. Tony came through with his bodyguard friend. It took some time for me to trust him, but Tony made it easy by checking on both of them when I continued to keep under Chrome.

It was the weekend when I decided to make moves on my plan. I went to the Jazz club sat in a closed secluded area watching everyone and everything going on. I learned a lot about the dope business sitting pretty up under Chrome. His schooling was for me to carry on in case something should happen to him. He wanted me to take over his domain in Liberty City streets. I knew how to watch the butt ass naked girls chop up the dope and bag it, he had a money machine but nothing like counting it yourself if you ask me, and he had me checking the merchandise both weak shit and the good shit so I would know the difference. Being the strong woman I am that white brick never took me. Mary Jane was more my preference. When you first walk in to the club, you get a vibe feeling, but through the eyes of an upcoming dealer, you learned your surroundings and the people in it. I watched for users, and how the regulars knew to go up to the bartender handing them folded up big bills for a closed hand slip of a speed ball, or a ¼ gram of coke.

My mind soaked in every detail, and I was going to use it to run the Keys. Not running into Chrome's territory but instead take from him what he thought he had control of. Six Two may have been Chrome's right hand but he also was waiting for Chrome to give him his own piece of the game, his own dynasty to take over in lil Havana, little did he know that wasn't in Chrome's plan. This was going to be easier than taking candy from a baby.

CHAPTER 10 LA MUERTA

My first move was to get a lot of money. I went to the bank and handed in my resignation, Boss man was not happy to see my pretty ass go, but I had to cut ties, because what I was about to do was either going to compromise me any way or I would have to make a run for it and leave. If I had to start my life over in a new place I would still need references, and Boss man was always good to me. I closed my checking's account, savings account, my total shares, and had my broker cash out one of my IRA accounts, all totaling a little over three hundred seventy five thousand dollars. I told you your girl really had her own. I left the money that Kat and I deposited in the off shore accounts for rainy days which from the dope game totaled seven hundred seventy five thousand dollars of what I haven't spent. Thanks again to Chrome's idiocy of showing me around to all his connections and hook ups, I wouldn't have a problem starting off with what I needed as far as protection. His so called boys were checking me out behind his back, so it was easy for me to walk up in the gun range, sweet talk P.A. and leave with a nice twelve gage shot gun, and two magnums and his private cell number, who knows it might come in handy.

Tony drove with me to the Key's and we got a warehouse off of Islamorada exit near the boat docks. It was dark and secluded, perfect for me to run business out of. I plopped my duffle bag on the long benched table to unpack my gear.

"What you got in that bag of tricks Brook? Anything for me?" Tony asked me being his normal goofy self.

"I got what I need, and no there is nothing in here for you. This is where we separate our ways Tony. Listen, thank you for all you have done for me and Kat these past few weeks, but this is personal, and it's my mess to clean up. I can't have you around when this shit goes down. Heat still wants your head on a platter, so you need to get out of Florida for a while. Here take your Mom and little brother to the Cayman Islands for a few weeks, I'll give you heads up when it's safe to come back, but if you don't hear from me DON'T COME BACK!"

I had to be straight with Tony, I handed him three plane tickets, keys, and a brochure to the hotel I booked in advance for their stay on the Island.

I couldn't have him in this anymore. On the table also laid out bullets, shot gun shells, a blond wig, and big dark Vera Wang shades to disguise myself and leave Brooklynn behind to be La Muerta, which means death. I needed a name Chrome and his crew would not give it a second thought.

"I don't know Brook, you are going against some real dangerous people here. I can't just leave you here to take this all on your own. This isn't a game, you can really get hurt or even killed. Look at what happen to Kat, they might do worst to you. I am staying." Tony with his protective coat of armor tried to talk me out of sending him away. It was getting annoying though. If he stayed I wouldn't only have me to worry about bout, I would have him as well, but I know Tony can be very stubborn when it comes to me, I would have to get creative.

"You think you are helping, but I can't make you go either. Tell you what; take your family to the Islands once they are safe I'll send for you to come back. I won't make a move without you here. OK?"

I hope I would be persuasive enough for him to fall for it. As soon as he get there, I wouldn't call him, text him, nothing. He would just have to chill his ass on the Island.

"Fine Brook, but you better not do a thing til I get back." He warned me, but in a cute way. Once Tony was out the picture and Kat was safely hidden I texted P.A. to hook me up with a couple of loyal goons for my own protection in the Key's. Kat was helpful too once I sat down and told her my plan, only she knew exactly what was about to go down. If I had told Tony he would only bitch up and try to shut my operation down before it even started. He only knew what I wanted him to know. Kat told me about a hot Latina Contessa from Puerto Rico that she knew, of course personally, but I didn't ask for the bedroom details. Anyway the Contessa agreed to meet me, and once she saw Kat, I guess a whole lot of happy memories came back to her, because she did not hesitate to supply me with some high grade Sour Diesel and twenty bricks. It didn't take long for the tourists and Key West Natives to get hooked on my shit. I had small timers, and even some strippers selling for me.

Everyone in the Key's was getting hooked on that La Muerta. Now, I was getting somewhere, and soon Six Two would pick up my scent and when the timing was right, I would lure him in for the kill.

CHAPTER 11 GETTING INTO BED WITH THE ENEMY

Living a double life was no easy task, especially when one life had to be with Chrome. Chilling with him, kissing him, sleeping with him was making my blood crawl at times, but I had to do it to keep him near.

"B, is everything all right? I feel you been a little distant these days." Chrome walked out of the steamy bathroom with his burgundy towel that had his monogram on it, and asked me as I was sitting up in the bed watching the news. I just wanted to pull the cover over my eyes so I wouldn't have to endure looking at his deceitful being.

"Yeah everything is good babe, I just been swamped with all these wedding preparations." I answered him like a good wife to be. That was my cover for the time away from him when I had to hold up being La Muerta. He would think I was out planning this big wedding for us.

"If it is too much stress I can come with you and help make some plans. Better yet, how about you invite your Mom for the weekend and y'all can do a lot from here and I will have a Wedding Planner come to you." He continued to try and figure me out while he got dress in his business suit, which can mean only one thing that he was going to meeting, maybe with Heat. I almost forgot about Heat, He was the main source of all the bull shit that came down on Kat.

"I don't remember you telling me you had plans today? I thought we could spend the day together." I lied to him to see if he will tell me where he was going, or take me for that matter.

"Oh my bad B, but yeah I have a meeting today, and this dude crying about some Spanish Ho he think coming to take his money."

"Sounds like he bitching up to me, I don't see why you fuck with bitch ass crack heads anyway. Listen I know y'all bout to be boring my ass to death, but I really want to spend more time by your side learning how you deal with these ass holes, so give me a minute I will come with you." I left no room for Chrome to shut me out of this meeting, I know when I was with Tony, Heat couldn't keep his eyes off of me. He whispered once to me that I was too ladylike to be around Tony and these other bitches he would have at his party. So flaunting my sexy ass in front of his slimy ass Irish wannabe but know he from Tennessee, having everyone else do his dirty work today might get him to bite the hook I have waiting for his trifling self. He just might get his wish to meet La Muerta sooner than he thinks.

"That may not be a bad idea, I love the way you have come around on getting into my world with me B. I can see us now, Bonnie and Clyde of the street hustle. Go get dressed and I'll meet you down stairs." Chrome was fooling himself about us being down for each other. He killed that life line between us, and he would soon see how it all falls down.

An hour later and yes, I made him late for his meeting waiting for me to get all glamour out, wearing a sexy white halter evening dress that exposed my beautiful back and ruffled down my legs to the front. This dress was perfect fit to show off my curves and have Heat eyes dangling like shark bait...

"Are you ready to go?" I asked Chrome, coming down the stairs towards him in the foyer where he was standing smoking a cigar waiting patiently for me.

"Damn B, you look so good I just want to take you back upstairs, fuck the meeting tonight." He said wiping drool off the side of his mouth.

"Now that would not be business like, we are professionals remember. Besides there will be plenty of time for you to take this off of me later."

I told him, bringing him back to the terms of how we roll. With no time to waste, we headed off in Chrome's black Mercedes Benz to meet with Heat.

When we got to Heats oversized mansion on Ocean Drive in Miami, I noticed Six Two's dark sedan parked outside. It had me wondering why the hell does that seem shady to me but not Chrome, I knew Six Two was trying to get from under Chrome, the way he was doing it though will bite him in the ass later. As we walked up to the front doors where Heat had two body guards waiting to allow us in, I took a mental note of how many peeps he had around his house protecting his skinny assets. Chrome reached out for my hands walking in, his way of feeling like a King and Queen representation, which I oblige to for the moment. Heat was in his living room looking quite a disgraceful mess, he is such a coke whore.

"What took your ass so long to get here Chrome, I told you this was some serious shit I need to talk to you about, and you took your sweet fucking time."

Heat was disrespecting Chrome to the fullest, but I reflect off of Chrome, so that shit won't slide with me, but as I was about to go ham on Heat's ass Chrome put his hand out to pause me, he felt my rage and knew he needed to step up and take over.

"Hold on now Heat, I'm here now, so calm your hyper ass down, get you another drink and let's talk."

I have to give it up to Chrome for how he handled his ass just now. Smooth talker was his thing, he knew exactly what to say and how to say it to make anyone feel they were in good hands with him, but in my case I wasn't safe with him.

"Ahright ahright ahright, let's just sit down and talk this thing out. I'm sorry where are my manors, Brooklynn, right? You want a drink baby." Heat greeted me now getting a good look at my ass, once he calmed down, came over me kissing my hand, like a charmer dude. I'll let that shit slide for now. Chrome and I sat down on the dark walnut leather couch and Six Two was chilling in the background on a lazy boy chair.

"Now start from the beginning Heat, and don't get all worked up, cuz I ain't in the mood for that high pitch accent you do when your blood boils."

Chrome took control of the conversation while making himself comfortable on the couch waiting to hear Heat's complaints, as Heat signaled for one of his men to pour me a drink.

"I'm hearing bad shit dawg, all bad shit about some Latina bitch taking over in the Key's, what if she finds out that the Key's aint enough and come here to Miami to run shit. I hear her stuff is some quality shit too. I want her gone."

Once again Heat was ordering Chrome to do his dirty work for him. I wanted to assure his bitch ass that the last thing he needed to worry about was losing business, I was about to take his breath away.

"We run Miami. There is no threat of trespassers here. Let the bitch have the keys, if she makes anything of it, we will take her and have her working under us. You say she's Latino right? Well maybe we can even let her bring our shit back to her country and then we really would be on the map."

Chrome wasn't concerned with La Muerta taking over he saw it more as a business venture if anything.

"So you don't think we have anything to worry about. Good, good then, I leave it in your hands." Heat said calming down, but still taking drinks to the head allowing me to assume he was not thinking on the same level Chrome was. I sat there quietly observing his movements, his men movements, all the while holding my snifter glass in my hand dangling the big rock of diamond so that it caught Heats eyes. I crossed my legs that caused the slit in my dress to open up a little bit showing my thigh high. I saw that Heat was watching and I gazed sensually at him letting him think whatever he wanted to think. Chrome put his hand on my leg unconsciously at that moment, snapping Heat back to reality.

"That's all I'm saying Heat leave it to me, and if it makes you feel better I'll keep an open eye out for her. Now getting on some real business when is my next shipment coming in? I have a connected dock worker on my payroll, and he assures me that he is trustworthy to work with."

Chrome bringing light to their meeting with potential growth to their smuggling drugs from Panama.

"Now this is what I like to hear. Willis, the captain of the cargo ship that has my packages should arrive tomorrow night at 1:30 am at the dock so get your boy on it now. I checked in with him when he picked up at the drop off after the Coast Guards left. Here is the information." Heat informed Chrome about a *special cargo* shipment, handing him a slip of paper with all the details about the ships arrival, the Dock master, and the port number.

"Looking good, Heat my man. I need to call my boy now where can I go and make this call?" Chrome asked Heat to make a private call, guess he still like to keep some shit secretive. Here was my chance to pull out all the stops and get Heat indisposed.

"Go in my office, all the privacy you need." He pointed Chrome to the direction across the hall. Six Two followed behind Chrome to stand in front the door protecting his Boss man. I could see the look in Six Two eyes that it was killing him to keep being a go to for Chrome. But that was not my main concern now, right now was my only chance to get close to Heat.

"So I guess this leaves us two huh Heat?" I softly said to him sipping from my glass elegantly. Heat's eyes rose to mines.

"Wow Brooklynn baby doll, you have really grown into an extraordinary classy business like woman. Tell me something isn't life better for you with Chrome than with oh what's that lousy DJ name again Terry?"

Heat was not making it easy for me to get into character to seduce his ass, I wanted to slash his throat right then, knowing that Tony was the best DJ he ever known, but then I would have to kill all of these mother fuckers in here and that would definitely be hard since I didn't come prepared.

"Oh do you mean that Tony guy?" Terry, Heat's new flame for the moment answered. She could be expandable too, if she's not careful.

"Yeah Tony, that's his name, well Baby Doll, what's life like in the fast lane now?"

"I don't know yet, I thought you were the fast lane Heat, Chrome is merely the highway." I turned on my charmed voice and started to run my game on Heat's mindless nature.

"Ha ha, do you guys hear that? Brooklynn too bad your with Chrome, but if you ever stray away, you can always ride with me in the fast lane." Heat whispered in my ear, sitting next to me and getting an inhale of my N 5 Chanel essence. I looked at him and knew that was my open door.

"I'll keep that in mind." I replied short but sweet. He was getting more than he bargained for coming on to me like that.

When Chrome was done having his private conversation with his new lap dog, he shook hands with Heat, and we all headed out, including Six Two. That night I could barely keep my eyes close, listening to Chrome's hypnotic breathing while he slept like a baby after I gave him the fuck of his life when we got back. He couldn't wait to undress me, playfully we tangle with each other trying to be the aggressor in our four play of pleasure, all the mean while I wanted to be the giver, forcefully making him beg for more of me, I would give him a little and then take away a lot, he was thick and hard standing naked before me, I did enjoy fucking him when we were together, but now that he is my enemy I didn't look at this as pleasure, more like business, getting his guard down enough for me to slid up under him like a snake and strike for the kill when the time is right. I got out of bed, took a shower and texted Kat that I was coming over to see her. It was risky for me to talk to her or text her around Chrome but he was sleep now, and when he wakes up I will be already gone. I did bring up Kat in a conversation with him, just not to think of why I never wonder where she was, and when he replied that he hasn't seen or heard anything, I just shook it off and made a comment about her probably finding some rich Ho and getting herself caught up. It was my way of not setting off any alarms in his head.

Kat was wide awake as well when I got to her place, it was a relief to know that Tony's Body Guard was doing his job and keeping my girl safe. I hugged her so tight, and started to sob again when I look at her face, she was still swollen around her eyes, but at least now she can get up and move around. I guess the therapist was doing well with her.

"I hate having to leave you alone to go through all of this by yourself girl, but I promise it will soon be all over." I try to reassure her that she wouldn't have to live her life hiding. I was getting jittery too though, but I couldn't let her feel or see my fear, my thoughts were my own right now, and I have to be clear headed.

"I believe in you Brook, but what's up? It's like two in the morning, what are you doing here so early?" She asked concerned about my early visit to her.

"Where do I start Kat, I couldn't take one more minute laying down next to that sack of shit. I had to get out of there before I end up killing him earlier than expected and fucking up my whole plan."

I plopped down on her bed and laid back with my hand over my face of shame with what I had to do to keep in composure. Kat sat next to me on the bed with her legs cross Indian style like a little girl.

"Brook there is something I haven't told you about that night. I didn't want to tell you, because I can't believe it myself, but you don't know who you are dealing with."

I sat up immediately looking at Kat with a confused look. I thought she told me everything what was so bad she had to keep it a secret from me.

"Yes Six Two and his fucking disciples beat me, raped me, and left me for dead. What I didn't tell you is that Chrome was there too. He watched, as if to make sure they did what they were supposed to. He never blinked or tried to save me, he just stood there waiting for them to finish me off. That's the mental image I can't get out of my head, your man standing there waiting for me to die!" I sat there in shock, and even though my heart was already torn by Chrome sending his goons out to do the dirty deed for Heat, the fact he was actually there and could watch someone that he knew was dear to my heart being destroyed and then come home expecting to lay with me that same night broke my heart completely. I really did not know who I was in bed with. He was no longer a pawn in this he was the King I needed to take down for all he got.

"I am so sorry Kat that you felt you couldn't tell me this. Sisters for life remember that. No man will ever come between us again." Kissing her tears of hurt away, I left her knowing I will always have her back, and headed out the door. No more time to wait, it was now or never. I texted Heat to meet me at a motel that was near South Beach. It would be crowded and noisy there enough smoke to hide from the fire. I am pretty sure Heat would bring two of his men with him for protection in such an open scene, but I couldn't risk going to his house and being seen, besides, I also texted him not to say who he was meeting to no one, so that it wouldn't get back to Chrome just yet. He replied that he wouldn't and said he couldn't wait to taste my baby doll ass. He was going to taste something all right, but it wouldn't be my ass, it just might be the barrel of my gun. Wearing my Blond wig and my hat disguising myself as La Muerta, I found a veteran woman of the night around the block from the motel. I paid her two hundred dollars and gave her money to rent the motel room for me, and told her there was more money in it for her if she kept quiet about me tonight.

"I got you Mamacita, no one will know that I saw you tonight, you keep my pockets filled like this, and we got no problems." She replied with a big chewing gum smile on her face. I almost felt sorry for her constantly standing on those red tired looking pumps from walking up and down the streets waiting for a ride to change the stats of her night. Her face was all prettied up with make-up but it didn't do much to hide the bruise she maybe got from her pimp under her eye. Her once caramel skin that use to glow was now an ashy light brown color with no shine. All more the reason I picked her tonight, with the money I would lay out on her she can take a week off and rest a bit, or maybe feed her kids and not have to worry about tricks for a while.

"Here you go Mama, I got you the Presidential suite, even though that shit don't look like the President would stay there." She explained to me still smiling with rosy cheeks and plush pink lipstick smile. I saw pure innocence in her eyes, her body may have lied about her age, but her eyes told me she was only 19 years old.

"You did good lil Mama, what they call you?" I asked her, with a slight Hispanic accent so not to expose out of character, hiding my eyes behind my dark shades.

"Oh they call me Honey T, but my real name is Tiffany."

"Tiffany, that is a pretty name, how bout you take this two grand for helping me out and get off of your feet for a few days. One more thing, have a doctor check out that shiner on you, we wouldn't want that getting infected."

Handing her a money roll I took out of my purse, I showed my gratitude and hope she take my advice to go to the hospital. She took the money roll and blew a kiss to me as she walked off into the night, probably not adhering to my concern.

I quickly walked into the lobby of the Motel, keeping my head low so that the cameras would not catch a good picture of me. Once I got up to the top floor, and opened up the Presidential suite, I realized that Tiffany was not lying about this being a hell hole, more than a suite. At least it was clean, so I made do with what I had to work with. I was already dressed for the seduction part under my black trench coat. Opening my overnight bag, I took out a bottle of Patron, Heat's favorite drink, and poured it in two glasses, but I laced one with a sleep agent molly. After one drink he will be defenseless as I take him apart. Almost running out of time when I saw Heat's Blue Porsche pull up and his two men coming inside with him, I hid my hunters knife and my magnum with a silencer under the pillow, took off my coat, shades, wig, hat and put them back in my bag, and sat on the bed with my full c cup babies ready to influence his eyes. I sat patiently waiting but at the same time palms are sweating, I rub them on the sheets trying to get them dry, and then I saw the doorknob turn and heard the second card key he used to open the door that I told Tiffany to leave at the check in desk for him. He walked in and took one look at me as I sat on the bed pleasing to his eyes. He closed the door behind him quickly so not to let his goons see me, because I am sure they were right outside the door.

"Wow, you look fucking amazing, like I always pictured you without your classy dresses. Come here so I can get a good look at your fine ass." Heat said to me with Christmas gleam in his eye, coming up close and putting his hand out for me. I'll play the part for now. I gently put my hand in his, and stood up on my high heel black slick boots. He twirled me around and I paraded for him.

"How about I get us a drink to get a little more comfortable and loose?" I asked him intentionally to get this show over and done with. He nodded as I switched my sexy little ass wearing only a black g string and a halter top walking over to get the prepared drinks, holding his in my right hand and mine in my left.

"You know I always did have a thing for your Irish ass Heat. Now take this to the head so Brook Baby can give you exactly what you need to ease your mind."

I seductively sweet talk his cornball, cheap suit wearing, faded blond hair looking self. His cheap cologne was giving me a migraine, but he obeyed my every demand. He took the drink straight up, and then his dumb ass pulled out a stash of coke and did two lines up his pointy nose. A major turn off for me.

"There I go again, no manors. Do you want a line Baby Doll? I've got plenty on me."

Heat offered me some of his party favors, with traces of white powder under his nose. I shook my head to him and vaguely smiled at him.

"Tell you what my Irish King, I have another surprise for you, I am going to the bathroom to get it ready, you just get undress and ready for me."

I said to him sinfully smiling, thinking how sweet this is going to be. He raised his hand and waved in the air, oh yeah that drink was kicking in, and soon he will be out like a light. He went to do another line but I had to take it from him, it would do more damage than help right now.

"You know what I was being rude. I think I will have a line after all."

I persuaded him to give it up to me, I picked up the little mirror he had it on to take to the bathroom, when I turned to walk away, and he slapped me on my ass. I wanted to cuss his ass out.

"Yeah you do that sexy, and hurry the fuck on, my dick is so hard for you right now I'll be putting holes in these walls fucking your pretty ass."

His words were so romantic, I could just throw the hell up, literally I was feeling nauseous, and I don't know why. I wasn't feeling nervous about tonight no more, I shook off the feeling to get my head straight. I went to the bathroom and put on a pair of black jean shorts, and my V-neck red short sweater on, so I wouldn't have to waste time later getting dress. I put on my blond wig and brought out my bag to rest it on the dresser near the fire escape outside the window for a clean get away.

"Get ova herrrre nnnow...." That was Heats last words before he slipped into a slight unconsciousness yet conscious enough for me to say a few words to him.

"Heat, look at me.."

I was sitting on top of him now and I have him just where I want him. Slapping his face a little so he could wake up to hear and see me take away his life like he so easily order Kat's life away. He woke up looking at me with his drugged heavy eye's not understanding what's going on.

"C'mon Heat don't flake on me now, we just started the party. I want you to be a part of this you're the guest of honor. Well really your more like the slime ball of the year. I know all about your hit on Kat, but I bet you didn't know it was me who sent her to spy on you. Here's another thing I bet you didn't know, I am La Muerta, and you no longer have to look for me or worry about your precious dynasty, because you can't take it to Hell! You cock sucker mother fucker."

Heat had fear in his eyes when I let him in on the real deal of our late night rendezvous, guess I was right, he was no King Pin that's for sure. He began to shake his head no.

"What? No, What? No don't kill you, or no don't take your life away or let me guess no it wasn't you right? Heat I have been on to you since your bitch been sucking Tony's dick, oh and to answer your question, Tony was a better life for me. Just look at what life with Chrome has done to me. It brought me to kill you tonight." I said in a sarcastic tone. I pulled out my gun from under the pillow.

"Noo, don't don't kill me, I'm sssorry, don't-"

"Shhh, be quiet or I'll bitch slap you with this gun, now man the fuck up and take this shit. You lucky I don't ram this up your ass like you had Chrome and his Goons do to Kat. Don't worry you won't be alone in Hell for long, I will send you company soon. Buenos Noche' hijo de puta."

My pain, anger, and soul came out in my words to him, before I grabbed the pillow next to him and put it over his head and squeezed the trigger, killing him with one shot to the head. I began to laugh out loud as if we were having a good time, so not to set off his men from the quietness of his death. I then took out the knife from under his pillow and carve a special note on his chest. Turning on the TV to a porno channel, and raising the volume would keep the boys at bay until I get far enough from here through the balcony window. Before I left, I packed away all my weapons, and rinsed out the two glasses leaving no traces of my finger prints or lipstick. The one thing I did think about right after I got in my car that was parked in a garage around the corner, was where to go now. I needed to get home before Heats men find him and call Chrome. If I am not home Chrome will put two and two together. I stepped on it taking the back streets home zooming in and out of traffic, and slowing down whenever I see a cop car, the last thing I needed was to be stopped by a cop for a speeding ticket and if he finds loaded weapons in my car and a bloody knife. After driving for fifteen minutes, I finally got back to Chrome's crib. I took out the bag with my stuff in it, threw my wig and shades in it and then I hid it behind a bunch of bushes on the side of the house. The house was still in darkness which led me to believe that Heat had not been discovered yet. I went inside the house, and took out my cell phone I deleted every last text between me and Heat, I had took his cell phone and dumped it on the way home. There would be no links to me from him. I started to walk upstairs slowly and quietly, I peeked in the room, Chrome was all hugged up with my pillow knocked out still. I snuck past him and when I got to the bathroom, I closed the door, turned on the hot water in the shower to hurry and steam up the bathroom. I took off my boots and striped down my disgusting clothes that had Heat's scent all over it. Then I put it all in a bag and stuck it under the sink for now. I didn't start to tremble or playback in my mind the events that just took place of taking a man's life until I was under the hot water scolding my body as if it was my punishment. Even though it was a scum bags life, still it was not mine to take, but this was only the beginning because soon Chrome will be looking for who killed part of his income.

As I just stood under the brail of hot shower drops, Chrome walks in startling me.

"You want some company B? Last night was amazing, then again every moment with you is amazing."

He invited himself to my realm of shame. I was not really ready to face him, while my blood was still pumping hatred despising him.

"I was just about to get out, sorry I woke you up, I just couldn't sleep. It's been about three weeks now, and I still haven't heard or seen my girl." I protested to be distraught by the absence of my friend so that he wouldn't just know that it was him I was distraught to be around, his smell, his essence of beguile that taunted me, I wanted this to be all over and behind me.

"B, why are you bugging? You know that girl can take care of herself, and you know she will pop up out of the blue with one of her sexual lesbian escapades events to tell you about. How many times do I have to tell you baby, don't worry." He babbled on and on about Kat popping up, but in his mind he knew she was gone, and in my mind, I couldn't wait to see his face when I make her magically manifest to his funeral.

I pulled away from his arms holding me and got out of the shower, I ran the hot water so long I'm sure it will run cold on his ass in a minute. I put on my towel and headed to the bedroom. My head was pounding, and I was feeling sick to my stomach. I'm starting to think this is what people go through the first time they kill someone. Going over to my dresser, I pulled out my black panties and bra to put them on. I went into the closet to put on my jogging suit.

"OH SHIT!"

I heard Chrome yelled out, guess the cold water hit his ass good.

"Damn B, you used up all the hot water." As he came out to cry like a little bitch about some damn shower water, his phone began to vibrate like crazy. I closed my eyes still standing in the closet holding on to one of the rails as I began to feel sick to my stomach again.

"Now who the hell is calling me now this damn early?" He said sucking his teeth picking up his phone dripping wet all over the carpet with no towel on, just letting it air dry.

"What?" He answered the phone in rage. I came out of the closet to sit on the bed with my back facing Chrome who was on the other side of the bed, so that I can ease drop on the conversation without giving myself away.

"Wait, wait, slow the fuck down Man and start over." Whoever called him was in such a panic Chrome couldn't understand what the fuck they were saying.

"Alright, hold on I'm turning on the news right now." Chrome said, grabbing the control to his forty two inch high definition TV and turned it to channel 7 News.

"Yeah I'm watching it now." He continued his conversation, while watching the news.

"And now we join Mehgan on the scene."

"Thank you Belky. We are on the scene of what seems to be a brutal murder with a message. Richard Burns who goes by the name of Heat on the streets of Miami, was found shot in the head. Witnesses say that he had a late night date that seemed to go sour. There was a strange marking on his chest done with what appears to be a Hunters knife. Two words "La Muerta" which means death was carved in his blood. This was definitely a homicide, and more to do with a deal that went bad."

"WHAT THE FUCK!"

Chrome shut off the TV before the news finished, and yelled over the phone. Guess he is not talking Heat's death well. This was only the beginning of Chrome's world crashing down.

"I'm getting dress now, I can't *believe* this shit here boy, and who you said was with him?......... Nah, what the fuck was they doing while he was getting his head blown off? I'm on my way don't do anything til I get there."

He demanded just before he ended the call. I couldn't move. I just sat there trying not to even breathe too hard in fear of telling on myself with my actions.

"What the hell was Heat doing in that part of Miami anyway? This doesn't make any sense. Brook Baby I got some bull shit to go handle." Chrome barely acknowledged me with his news about Heat's passing. I was in the clear. It was time to put on the wifey routine, and console his sorry ass.

"Awwe I'm sorry Babe, damn that shit is crazy, we were just with Heat, and everything seemed to be good. Listen take all the time you need, I have some errands to run today, and I'm meeting Mom to go over wedding plans. So don't worry about me." I said giving him an excuse to stay out all day and night. Besides, I needed some time away from him again. Going to Kat's place would give me that piece of mind.

"Thank you B, you always know what to do to make things right. Here, take this and get whatever makes you happy for the wedding. I'll call you later."

Chrome handed me about ten thousand dollars from his top draw in a money clip where he kept his pocket change. I took it from him even though I had way more in my bag. He finished putting on his black slacks, shirt, and a jacket. He grabbed his keys off of his Armoire, kissed me on the cheeks, and left like the wind. As soon as I heard his car screeching down the driveway, life came back into my body. I hopped up off the bed, grabbed the clothes from under the sink in the bath-room that had Heats blood on it and I went downstairs, threw it in the fireplace and lit it on fire. After I made sure the fire was out. I grabbed a small suitcase, packed some clothes and jewelry. Never leave without the jewelry. I grabbed my keys, said goodbye to my partial home, ran to the side of the house and picked up my duffle bag, threw everything in the back seat and I hauled ass to Kat's condo.

CHAPTER 12 DO OR DIE

On the way to Kat's, so many things run through my mind, more like questions. Was this the only way out? Am I forgetting anyone that could come back for revenge? Do I really want an explanation from Chrome about his part in this? Questions that may never be answered especially when I have already put things in motion. There was nothing left to do but to finish what I started.

Before I got out of my car, my phone started to vibrate, it was Chrome texting me.

Just wanted to thank you again baby for understanding luv you, your Future Hubby..

I shook my head revolted by the very thought of him. Taking the duffle bag with me to Kat's condo, once again it made me smile to see a trust worthy guard in front of her door. I greeted him as he opened her door for me.

"Hey Brook honey, look at me." Kat greeted me when I walked in with the best surprise ever, she was back on her feet walking with a pimped out cane to help her instead of the hurtful stuffy looking cruches from the hospital. I was so relieved to see my girl looking high spirited, even with her *pimp cane.*

"Look at you girl, you're hot and on fyah with your sexy ass cane." I said to her in my pleasing voice.

"Yeah I know, nursey got this fo me, she had it custom made check this out."

Kat explained to me as she pulls apart the cane handle that was shaped like a gold mermaid from the stick and turned it into a sword. I was amazed but it did suit her.

"I am glad to see the nurse is taking great care of my girl, and making sure you have protection in such a designer way." I said with admiration for the extent that the nurse took to make Kat feel safe. Looking at the cane you can tell a great deal of work went into making it.

"Yes, she is doing her thing, but enough of about my good news, what are you doing here so soon Brook? I wasn't expecting you til tomorrow. Is everything ok?" Kat was concerned about my early arrival. She limped as she walked over to her coach leaning on her cane to one side, preparing herself to rest a bit.

"I don't even know where to begin. There is no way to say this, so I'll just say it, I killed Heat last night, and I thought that I would be ok, but I got this pain deep in the pit of my stomach. I'm not cut out for this Kat."

"Oh Honey, it will be alright. C'mon we can do this, he deserved it. Weren't you the one always telling me and showing me that we can't stay in the dark? Well now is that time for us to shine. Fuck a Bonnie and

Clyde, girl we be Thelma and Louise all the way til the end. That feeling you getting in your stomach, that is your fearless soul, you wouldn't be human if you felt nothing after killing him. Just remember we in this together, but if we don't finish it, they will catch on, and come back to finish the job. I need you Brook."

Kat was sounding more like me, and she was right, we were in this together, and I can't bail on her like I did that night.

"Damn girl, when did you get so gangsta on me?" I asked her smiling and getting my balls back intact.

"When you saved me and brought me back to life." She selflessly answered taking my hand into hers and put it over her heart. Right there and then the fear and nerves went away, and the strength and courage kicked in. Back on track, are my thoughts now;

"Ok let's do this, now it's time to get Six Two vulnerable enough to get him away from Chrome, and I think I just might now how to do that." I proclaimed with confidence of a full proof scheme that Six Two wouldn't walk away from.

"Well I hope you include me on this one Brook, nothing would heal my wounds faster than to be the one to bring Six Two's world apart. My body wasn't fully recovered to be there for you with Heat, but I assure you my body is ready and willing, and we will do both Six Two and Chrome together."

The way Kat put things in perspective; I knew talking
her out of it would be no good. She had her mind set,
and she deserves to see this to the end as well. Put her
soul at ease.

"Here's what we will do."
I began to lay out the plan of my scheme to get Six Two.
Kat listened attentively she smiled and added some of
her ideas as well. The only thing is that we needed to
act right away, not giving them time to mourn the death
of their fallen comrade, but instead strike while they
guards was still at a low. We both agreed that whatever
happens we won't go quietly, it will be blazing guns of
fire if it comes to that.

CHAPTER 13 A BEGINNING TO AN END

The plan that Kat and I came up with was simple, and if everything goes smoothly, it should be one to go down in the books. I got dressed up as La Muerta with my blond wig, and dark shades. Kat added some accessories to my themed alto ego. She gave me a pair of her black leather biker girl gloves, leather pants, and a hot red shirt with a ruffle front, I also put on a black shoulder gun holster for my guns. With my new gangsta pinstripe fedora hat to finesse my refinery look to create La Muerta, I was ready to go.

"You look so damn fine hot Mama. Okay, so listen text me as soon as he takes the bait, I will be in the area in case anything goes wrong." Kat assuring me she had my back. I nodded to her before hugging her one last time and then we both headed out the door. She had her body guard with her, making me feel safe for her. I pulled up at Casanova's around seven p.m. before it got real crowded. Kat with her cell phone on was parked near by the club. When I walked in things were looking good when Carl didn't even know who I was when he greeted me at the door, I didn't say too much to him except that I wanted to sit at the bar, with a Puerto Rican accent. The lady bartender walked over to me wiping a glass with a towel and asked,

"What can I get you to drink tonight hun?"

"I'll take a brandy." I replied to her still portraying my Hispanic act. She came back with a half full sifter glass of brandy and a napkin.

"Can I get you anything else?" She asked me politely, smiling at me with my shade glasses on. At this point I refuse to remove my glasses. I felt more mystiques in them.

"As a matter of fact honey, there is something you can do for me. I'm looking for a guy they call Six Two, do you know him?"

I asked her pretending not to know who he is or what he look like, but I knew she knew him. She has been employed here for years, and was one of the best bartenders that Carl ever hired.

"Yeah I know him, what of it?"

"I am going over there to the table in the corner, when he comes in, ask him to join me, and here, this is for your troubles." I said to her, and then putting two hundred dollars tip for her on the bar. She nodded to me understanding and slid her polished nail tips over the money and pocketed it. Four hours, twenty minutes, and a bottle of Brandy later, Six Two and his goons finally walked their asses in the club. They came without Chrome, who had texted me earlier that he was going to see his hook up at the docks, which meant that Six Two was off for the night, and all mines for the taking. I watched him from my table that had low light above me only showing a shadow of a body and a hat. Six Two and his two followers were chilling at the bar. The Bartender gave me a quick glance and then glanced

over to Six Two letting me know that he was here. I
then tip my hat to her of acknowledgement. She headed
over to him and his crew and leaned over Six Two.

"You're being requested by that lovely lady over
there, and she even bought you a drink." She relayed
the message to him nudging her head in my direction
and placing a smooth cognac drink in front of him. He
took the drink and sipped it, and then headed in my
direction with his boys following. I pulled out a Cuban
cigar and held it to my dark velvet red lips; Six Two
leaned in with a lighter and lighted up my cigar. He
then sat down at the table putting his lighter back on
the inside of his suit jacket.

"I heard you were looking for me. The only people
that come looking for me are either trouble or business,
which one is you?"

"Oh well, we don't want any trouble now do we?
No, this is business for now." I replied with a little edge
in my voice and accent to throw him off.

"And what would that business be? Oh wait, I've
heard about you, you're that chick La Muerta. Man
you got some cojones coming over here to our hood. As
a matter of fact killing you right now might be very
good for me." Six Two was being cocky in his all mighty
position right now with Heat gone setting his gun on the
table, but I was about to crush his dream.

"I wouldn't say that it would be good for you,
because from what I hear is that you are Chrome's lap
dog, and the only thing you would accomplish by killing
me is putting Chrome higher on the food chain while

you do his dirty work. Look, I could care less about your little city here, I have bigger business out of the country, but knowing that I can make acquaintances before I leave is better for me. That way I can call on favors when needed."

I indulged in my heavy Spanish accent but was getting tired of Six Two slow ass not getting the hint.

"I see you, but what's in it for me, and what makes you think that I would work with you behind my Man's back." Six Two stated, but I could see right through his scheming ass, he needed this, he wanted a reason to turn on the one person who gave him status, he was going to bite the hand that fed him all these years.

"I am not the one who needs to prove anything. I have my status as you can see, and before you think about putting a bullet in me, take a look around, and notice that I got four deep in this bitch, so before you can even pull your trigger you and your boys will be laid out before my feet." I grilled up my face and spoke with a demeanor unknown to Six Two coming from a female thug. Taking a sip from my sifter glass showing no fear and waiting for him to make his move, I already had him at check mate.

"Say I do this, thing for you, I want to be the one to run the Key's as well as the whole South of Florida, can you make that happen?" He took the bait, line and sinker, and I grinned at his greediness to get to the top any shameless way he could.

"If you are trust worthy and handle making a trade for me, then yes I can make that happen for you.

Everyone in the South will know Six Two run things now."

"Ok, I'm in." He jumped to get in on the action without hesitation. I gave him a slip of paper about the supposed trade off meeting of when and where.

"I will have one of my men hand you a briefcase with one point five million dollars in it outside when you leave. Make the trade off with no casualties and you're good." I said to him signaling one of my men with my finger waving to the door, so he knew it was time to get the briefcase. I don't trust him at all but I knew one thing I could trust is that he was all about getting his own name, so if he believed in this deal, Kat and I were set to make it happen.

"Where do I meet you after?" He asked before standing up to leave.

"We will meet at a warehouse down by the docks. Now remember I want no casualties, and the meeting goes down in about four hours." I instructed him and he nodded in agreement. After that we went our separate ways.

Kat and I met up right after the meeting with Six Two. Her body guard was insisting on coming with us, but we were head strong on doing this alone. This part was our fight. The only thing we needed from him was to borrow his 1998 Monte Carlo. Then we drove out to Alligators Alley and parked off of the ramp near where Tony and I found Kat. We began to strap up and mentally prepare ourselves for what was going to be a night that changes everything for us. We waited patiently and went over our plan so many times that Kat had to stop me.

"Girl we don't have to do this if you don't want to. We have a shit load of money Brook, and we can just disappear."

She was trying to give me options, but she couldn't hide the hurt in her eyes, she needed me to pull my shit together, she needed me to finish this.

"I can do this, I'm good, and we're good. No turning back now." I assured her, leaving no room for disappointing virtues. She smiled at me, and kissed my hands, and off into a short distance I saw high beam head lights coming off of the road towards the spot.

"It's showtime." I whispered to Kat. When Six Two car rolled up and parked, I waited for him to get out. It took him awhile before he stepped out of his car, I guess he realized where he was, but not to delay him any further I turned on my headlights and got ready to get out, but then Kat grabbed my arm.

"Brook, there is four of them including Six Two, it was only supposed to be two." Kat said startled by Six Two riding four deep.

"It is ok, I got this, just you stick to the plan and wait for my cue." I told her, with a straight look in my eyes, letting her know that I could handle the inconvenience. I stepped out of the car leaving her inside, and walked towards the four men crew. Guessing that his conscience must have been fucking with him, when he realized where he was standing, his men had guns in their hands standing at ease waiting for his go head, but when he saw me, he looked at them nodding his head that it was ok allowing them to relax and put their heat away leaving them vulnerable.

"So what was this? Initiation or some shit like that. You trying to feel me out, see if I'm trustworthy?"

Six Two asked me as I stood before them, waiting for answers. When I surprised his ass by pulling out my two .357 magnum guns, (pewsh pewsh p pweshhh) and started shooting with no warning. Killing the two goons behind Six Two with one shot to the heart each, and then killing the third guy who was to the right of Six Two with two shots, one to his hand preventing him from pulling out his glock nine, and one to the chest laying him straight out. I have been mastering my aim at the range. (pewsh pewsh) two last shots, shooting out Six Two's knee caps, literally brining him to his knees. I walked up to him still aiming straight at him, because of my sneak attack up on his ass he was in a shock mode, not even reaching for his gun. Placing one of my guns back into my holster I reached inside his jacket taking out his gun leaving him naked from protection. He looked up at me still confused and pissed as he gripped his bloody knees with his hands. I step back a little still aiming at his head, and I followed his eyes as he watched a second figure approaching from behind me. He stared in disbelief at his own destiny before him. He had to know it was the end, when he realized a piece of his own work came back from the dead to haunt him.

"KAT!!"

He screeched out in a raspy voice realizing now what was going on.

"WHAT THE FUCK! I killed you, left your ass for alligator food. Damn Bitch you do got nine lives." He blurted out showing no remorse. He refused to bitch up for mercy.

"Yea, Six Two, Ima call you by your name give you some authority before you die so that when I take your last breath, your blood will be my new recognition in life. You punk mutha fucka, you just couldn't ask for my pussy, you had to devour it? I wanted to be the last bitch you see, so you can die shamefully knowing that a real chick took your life, not even an O.G. but some stripper you knew nothing about yet felt the need to obey a crack head. So now it's time to say goodnight Kat."

Kat showed him no mercy when she saw him close his eyes embracing his death as she took his glock nine out of my hand put it to his head and squeezed the trigger putting him out of his misery and gaining back her life at the same time. Four men laid dead by our hands, we have now gotten our hands dirty, even though Heat was my first kill, this one was more personal to Kat. She wiped her finger prints off of the gun and dropped it on Six Two dead body. Without a second thought Kat limped away and got in the car as if nothing happened. I took one last look and went in Six Two's car saw the briefcase full of my money and took it. Thinking to myself, only one thing left to do. We headed home.

The drive back was unpleasantly quiet. Really no need to talk, because even though it was one step closer for

Kat to have a life where she wouldn't have to look over her shoulders, the obstacles we have to jump through was weighing like a ton of bricks on us. When we got to Kat's condo, we sat in the car for a moment, and then we looked at each other. Call us crazy, but at the moment we busted out laughing. We laughed so hard,

"Bitch you really do got nine lives."

Kat mimicked in Six Two's voice entertained by the way Six Two reacted to her still being alive.

"and they say their goons. A real goon would have taken us out."

I said shaking my head then throwing it back on the head board of the driver seat, looking at Kat and still laughing.

"Well damn, if they are supposed to be Chrome's protection, then killing him should be without thought." I added in, yet couldn't help feeling a connection towards him.

After our good laugh in the car, we headed in the house. Kat went inside her bedroom to undress taking off her trench coat jacket and jeans that had Six Two's blood stains on it. I stayed in the living room taking out my guns and laying them on the table. Pouring me a stiff drink to relax my nerves was all I needed at that point.

"It's time." Kat came out of her room to remind me what I had to do next. I dreaded this moment, because in some twisted state of mind, the feelings I had for Chrome once was really strong and intimate, but now it

was time to shake that feeling and do what was
necessary. I pulled out my cell phone and texted him:

Hey babe, it's been quite a day with Moms,
Thought we could use a lil tlc time,
Booked a room at the Executive Hotel for just you and I
You can pick up the key at the front desk will meet you there
Tonight.

This would be the last text between Chrome and I. The
sun just started to come up, and I had a few hours to get
everything set up before he meets me at the hotel. I
took a shower, and felt so tired after it. How come I feel
so tired lately, and sick to my stomach? I questioned
myself, but couldn't come up with any answers except
this is all my nerves.

"You don't look so good Brook, here lay down and
rest up for tonight, I will take care of the set up. Don't
worry I won't go alone." Kat said to me taking notice
of how weak I seemed to be feeling. I laid down and
slept for what seemed like days to me, but only was
hours I realized when Kat shook me awake.

"Girl, I tried to let you sleep as long as I could, but
we are now running behind, it's 8:30 pm, and Chrome
will end up being there before us if we don't leave now."

"I can't believe I slept the whole day. What is
happening to me?"

"Don't sweat it, you just been stressed that's all, get
your ass up though and come on." I can tell the way Kat
sounded that she was ready to for all of this to be over.

Wasting no more time, I got up and put on my sexy slim black silk dress with slits on both sides, pulled my hair up off my shoulders in a floral puff bun, leaving two strands of my hair hanging down in a curl accenting my shoulders, and then I put on my smoky look make up on, with a black shade of lipstick. Slipping on my black stilettos I was looking fierce and ready to put on a show for Chrome.

I let Kat drive my jeep while I sat in the passenger side deep in thought about tonight's events, and scenarios of how things can go wrong, and what will I do if the moment occurs.

We reached in no time at the high class hotel right by the Miami Airport. Kat had made the arrangements for one of their exclusive suites with a Jacuzzi. Everything was thought of, down to Kat's disguise of a short black bob hairstyle wig, and dark tinted round shades. Her body guard was also helpful in providing her with a new identity and credit card to book the room under. In the end there were no ties to us.

"I ordered the dinner and had the nurse set it up for you, so we are good to go."

Kat spoke with determination in her voice, which scared me a bit that this whole life style has changed her. I didn't question her instead I understood her drastic change. We pulled up and parked off in the cut of the hotel, where it was the darkest of the parking lot, and then we got out and noticed that Chrome hasn't reached yet, which was a good thing. I went inside, and just like she said everything was set up right on time. The suite was prepared with a seduction and romantic essence. Sounds of bubbling champagne, steam from the Jacuzzi, music playing 'Say It' by Neo in the background setting the mood. My man was in for a big surprise.

As I began to pour champagne in the glasses, Chrome knocked on the door, I went over to opened it, and in his hands was a box of yellow Roses. He takes a look around and I can tell he was fascinated by how I took note in the details preparing a romantic atmosphere.

"Well, this is a surprise. You have laid out the very same dinner we had on our first date." His appreciation for my significant remembrance was just the ammunition I needed to proceed with my plans.

"Are these for me?" I asked taking the box of yellow roses as he passes them to me kissing me on the cheek.

"C'mon in big Daddy, and let me feed you, cater to you. Let your woman take care of all your needs tonight." Luring him in to a defeated position, I initiated my first chess piece move. He sat down awaiting my seduction.

First I gave him a bite of the peeking duck I had specially made for him, but he was distracted by my sensual appearance wanting to grab and grope me, however I needed him to eat, I needed him to get full for the night I had ahead of us.

"Chill Chrome Baby, and eat this for wifey, I promise there will be time for all that when I'm done feeding you." I told him giving him a shot of sake to drink.

"Ok, I see you B, I'm sorry for interrupting you, go on, do your thing to make Chrome Daddy happy." He said intensely, moving his hands away from me and on to his black suit pants grabbing his hard dick trying to hold it down from feenin for me. Picking up the chop sticks once again I went for the second dish to feed him, the Blow fish, and his favorite delicacy.

"Now open wide for me baby, it will leave a sweet devouring taste in your mouth." In my sexy low voice I prepared him for a taste of my endeavor to him.

He laced his lips over the chopsticks and sucked the delicate fish into his mouth. I watched him eat it, I watched him taste it, I watched him as he devoured it.

"I think it's time for desert now, don't you?"

I kept my charade of this intimate night going, and headed for the bedroom to get ready for the finally.

"OH SHIT! That's what I'm talking about, get that ass ready for Big Daddy." Chrome shouted out to me, and I can hear the sound of his belt buckle making me assume he is taking off his pants. I was in the room for about three minutes before I heard the sound of glass breaking on the floor.

That was my cue.

Shaking my head, walking back into the sitting room area, there he was, laying on the floor paralyzed with bubbles foaming at the sides of his mouth.

"Now see, this the shit I hate, when a punk ass bitch can't even control his bodily functions, and then you

going to expect me to clean your mess up." I badgered
him while he was in dispose, looking up at me confused
of why I am not trying to help him.

Standing before him fully dressed in my boot cut
jeans and black silk shirt, I pulled out a small vile bottle
that had the poison I used on his dinner which I fed to
him. I stooped down closer to him feeling sure he
couldn't touch me or hit me for that matter.

"You see this *Chrome Daddy*, this here is your
destination, I know, you are confused, so I will fill you
in." I began to tell him why he is in the position he was
in, just when Kat came out of the room, she had been in
there the whole time. I saw Chrome's eyes get wider,
giving me the impression that he thought she was dead.

"That's right, I found my girl, right where you and
your sorry ass crew left her for dead. Take a good look
at her now, she is outliving all y'all Motha Fucka's.
You have been lying to me all this time, but I think my
lie to you was better. You probably wondering why I
just didn't put a bullet into you like I did to Heat, oh
yeah, that was me "La Muerta", taking the one crack
head dude you just couldn't turn away from which led
you down this road, and my girl Kat took your boy Six
Two out, the BITCH you allowed to violate her, but
what I can't wrap my head around is how you didn't
give a fuck about how Kat's death would damn near kill
me when you stood there and watch them run train on
her. You're sick, you're worst then them you watched
and then came home to fuck me, but to your surprise I
wasn't home, did you really think I wouldn't find out?
Look at me when I'm talking to you." I slapped him

hard making his lip bleed as he look like he was about to let go of life.

"You made me into this lethal weapon, but you never put a safety on me to protect yourself. Guess what though, to show some kind of loyalty to your ass that you don't even deserve, I got a second vile here with me, just to put my mind at ease to know that I gave you a chance to save your own life. Too bad you're in dispose at the moment, by the way you have like a minute and a half left to take the antidote before there is no point of return for you. So, I will just leave it here on the table, and instead of saying good bye, how about *go to hell.*"

My good bye to him was justified, and I followed behind Kat walking out the door, but not before I heard a loud fumble that made me stop in my tracks, and then there was a dead silence. 'Bastard had a little life in him yet' I thought to myself, but it wasn't enough. Looking at my watch noticing his time was up. Kat was waiting in the passenger seat this time. We were all packed up with our suitcases, two briefcases of money, closed out all of our accounts in Miami, including renting out Kat's condo to her favorite nurse at a reasonable price, all she had to do was keep up with the bills. I thought we could use some new scenery while we let the heat in Miami die down. Getting ready to back out and leave this chapter of my life behind, I suddenly slammed my foot on the breaks, making the jeep jerk forward.

"WHAT THE HELL BROOK?" Kat screamed at me in total abrupt shock. But I couldn't help it, I had the sudden urge in my stomach to throw up, without responding to Kat, I rush to open the door and threw up right outside of my jeep. I sat back in the car when I was finished, and Kat had this dumb look on her face, and shaking her head. Coming to terms with her expression, a dark notion came to me as a stabbing knife to my heart.........

I had a seed growing inside of me, and Chrome planted it there.......... Kat put her hand over mind over my abdomen, and tears fell down my face.

Brooklynn Heat In Miami

About the Author

Lucy Cult, a Mother to five beautiful children, a Wife to high school sweetheart, a survivor of Cancer and a writer to all. "Chronicles of the Unlovable" is her debut book, which open doors for her to write three more novels coming out later this year and next. She has always love writing, and telling stories is her passion for life.